The New Inheritors

Also by Kent Wascom

The Blood of Heaven
Secessia

The New
Inheritors

Kent Wascom

Grove Press
New York

FIRST EDITION

Published simultaneously in Canada
Printed in the United States of America

First Grove Atlantic hardcover edition: July 2018

This book was set in 12.5 pt Garamond Premier Pro by
Alpha Design & Composition of Pittsfield, NH

33614080663379

ISBN 978-0-8021-2817-1
eISBN 978-0-8021-6569-5

Library of Congress Cataloging-in-Publication data is available for this title.

Grove Press
an imprint of Grove Atlantic
154 West 14th Street
New York, NY 10011

Distributed by Publishers Group West

groveatlantic.com

18 19 20 21   10 9 8 7 6 5 4 3 2 1

For Alise, always

Of all that was done in the past, you eat the fruit, either rotten or ripe.

—T. S. Eliot

PART 1

What You Do Not Know

Is the Only Thing You Know

1890 – 1895

One

He was born filled with animals.

Before he could see and before the gift of speech, before his hand could grasp the tools to channel them, to let them leap out onto canvas or page, the animals were there. They owned his proportions and made themselves known in his cries and movements and they prowled in the wet, dark Eden of his heart.

When their chorused noises woke his mother in the night, she, little more than a girl herself, would lay her ear to his chest and hear hoofbeats on grass and the seventeen-year whirr of locusts, the wingbeats of egrets rising from a field. The sounds of her girlhood in the piney woods of Mississippi, the place she had abandoned for the city of New Orleans and a man who was killed in a brawl not three months after she'd fallen pregnant by him. The man had barely acknowledged her pregnancy except to say what he wanted the child called if it happened to be a son, but he was dead and so she'd granted herself the privilege. She named him Isaac.

She lay awake in the small bed of her tenement room and listened as her baby gathered air and shot a wail from his lungs that shook her skull as though she were the one newborn, the cry echoing through the thin ceiling to the room above, where a woman lived who loved her.

When the time of the birth had come it was the woman from upstairs who rushed to the girl's bedside. The woman's name was Neda, an immigrant from the Balkans by way of Cyprus, where she'd grown up with the sharpest edges of the crescent and the cross pressed to the throat of her life. For the past year she'd worked alongside the pregnant girl in a row of forty others at the Indian Queen Cigar Co., off Decatur Street, rolling leaves until her knuckles locked and her wrists swole double. Neda had little English, but the girl learned to anticipate the woman's glances and the way she smiled when they stood before the basin scrubbing their yellowed hands at the end of a ten-hour shift. Learned that whenever she said the woman's name, Neda's throat would hitch and the brown pits of her eyes would shimmer with a slick of want.

The girl was not in love, never had been, as far as she knew, but just the same she could sense the force of the upstairs woman's desire, and she came to love the power that knowledge gave, to hold another's heart like hair snatched in her fist. And, besides, she was glad to not be alone. Glad for a body in bed beside her whose radiant need seemed to channel off the fear she had for that other body, the one inside her, growing and unknown. Then the night of the birth came and she was more than glad Neda was there, talking in her riven English, wiping vomit from the girl's chin, and pulling her upright into a squat when the birth went long. Laying hands on her hips, rubbing with the waves of pain.

Neda had known children to be born in silence, but this was a loud country and a loud birth. When it was over and the girl, spent and voiceless, tried to tell her what to do with the cord and the sac, where to bury them and how, Neda could only half make out what she said before the girl pitched back exhausted with the baby on her chest and would say no more. So Neda cleaned the chipped shears she'd used and carried out the afterbirth in her apron and emptied it into the canal a block away. What water meant for anyone's fate, Neda didn't know. Back in the room, the girl thought with fugitive sadness how, if the flesh of his first home and the cord that kept him there weren't buried in the earth, the child that lay between her breasts was fated to wander far and die young.

Though the girl understood this as certain truth, at times Neda would raise the baby to the lamplight and examine him for contrary signs. Cupping head and rump, she would look him up and down from bright blue temple veins to the black knot at his belly, the baby's eyes resisting the light, pinched face refusing everything but the breast that does not want him, and, prying open the child's hands, Neda would see written in the lines of his palms a bird's vision of the rivers and creeks that fanned across the region of his birth, the upper reaches of the coastal rim which spreads south in peninsular wings that shatter into island chains, enclosing the Gulf of Mexico. A place that is drowning or is already gone. The country under the country you may know.

—What are you looking for? the girl would say, leaning up in bed.
—Where he's going, who he'll be.

Two

Three days after giving birth the girl returned to work on the factory floor, baby tied to her back with a shawl, her loins swaddled with rags to catch the bleeding. The girl persisted in this for almost a year, Neda never far from her, always ready to take the baby, until one day the girl fell in with the roving congregation of a man who knew when the world would end and how. The answer was soon and in flames, and as she listened to this man and his followers shouting prophecy through megaphones and rolled up newspapers in the street below, she felt a tug at her soul. Her bent fingers were stayed for a moment by these high rhythmic voices of the inland South, hilltop echoes drowning out the regular drone of the lector who read to the workers from a boring novel about an orphan made good. Voices that called to the part of her that knew the truth of miracles.

Taken for dead at the age of seven, she'd been thrown into a quick-limed pit with other victims of that year's fever, awakening to the blank

6

white sky of her burial shroud pattered with the rain of dirt that sifted down through the tangled bodies of her family. At the sound of her screams the cousins who'd been tasked with digging the grave dove in and hauled her up through mother, sisters, brother, father, grandma, and cut her free. She was the last of the Golemans, a family rumored to be Jews or Indians depending on your source, and as it happens with lone survivors she was hard-pressed to see beyond herself and whatever calamity was coming next. Now she was caught in one of those upwells of religious fervor that mark the end of centuries. And so in the spring of 1891 she packed herself and her child off with some seventeen others (girls, maiden aunts, and widows) for a former convalescent home in the panhandle of Florida, just south of Tallahassee, where they would wait in the damp and the heat for the fire to fall.

Love-wracked Neda, who neither believed nor disbelieved, followed. She bought a ticket with her last week's pay and rode at the back of the congregation in the third-class car they took across the coast, feeling the culminate ends of her actions with all the resignation and mystery of something undertaken in a dream. She did it for the same reason she held the child when its mother wouldn't, because it was all she could do. But she never doubted the rightness of it. Like the god the girl believed in, love has its own conscience. When you hear the voice that speaks and commands, even against all sense and self-interest, you will either wither slow and die in denial of it or without guilt burn everything behind you and go. At such times love shouts louder than reason.

◆ ◆ ◆

The place they called Rising Souls lay on the western bank of the Wakulla River in an area of slash pine and sawgrass and temperamental karst given to sinks that swallowed houses whole and to mineral springs. At the center of its dozen acres, a pair of screen-windowed bunkhouses framed one such spring, into whose waters the tuberculars and rheumatics had been urged several times a day in the camp's previous life. Farther toward the river was the cottage that had once housed the superintendent and his wife, and now became the home of the Teacher, as he was known, and whosoever at the moment was in need of his pastoral care. Farther still, a hundred yards into the woods, in a patch that caught the sun and moonlight well, lay the graves of those patients who the waters had failed.

On the day of their arrival most were too dazed and weary to do much more than knock the rust and cobwebs from the bedsprings in the bunkhouse, beat out mattresses that had curled stiff like the silverfish and centipedes that rained out of them with each blow. Meanwhile, the Teacher took a place beside the water at the heart of the place and waited until everything was unloaded and the wagons and drivers they'd hired out of Tallahassee had headed out, far past earshot, to call his followers together.

He was a tall man, the Teacher, heavy, and with a smooth, round face whose chief feature was a red mouth that pursed frequently into satisfied smiles. He claimed to be from California and to have visited Jerusalem some years ago. The core of his teaching was that in order to hasten the joyous end and secure their place among the chosen, his followers must return to the state of what he called natural grace.

So once the women had gathered in a weary sweaty huddle at the spring, the Teacher drew off his every article of clothing (a condition in which some of the widows hadn't even seen their husbands) and, easing down the steps until the water was at his waist, bid them do the same. Neda stood dumbstruck beside the girl, who, passing her child to Neda and without hesitation, let her dress fall to her feet and went to the man in the spring. Neda, holding the child who bowed his back and tried to shove away, a compass needle pointing ever motherward, bore slack-jawed and horrified witness to what followed: The others went down, one by one, taking the Teacher's outstretched arm and letting themselves be led into the water. The soft mystery of algae furred the stone steps beneath their bare feet, whose soles had been hardened in truck patches and cottonfields; and some of the women slipped and caught and held each other in balance, their long braids snaking behind them in the water through the bright green skim of plant life, and then they were bobbing, buoyed. They struggled for balance as the spaces between them filled with lilies the size of dimes and ticking waterbugs and whirlers, more practiced dancers than themselves here in the wet. Not far from the pool, in the shade of a red maple, the smaller children watched their mothers and older sisters rise and fall. Neda went and sat among them, holding the bucking boy, the sweat in her eyes burning the vision of gleaming pale shoulders, darkened hair slicked with green as the Teacher put his hand to each of their heads. In Neda's lap, the boy was nudging, reaching out with the sustained urgency of children, for what he could not have, and it was like a part of her soul lay there squirming. Enough to hold herself together, much less this. Now the women and girls in the water sang together, a close, wordless harmony, floating, weightless for the first time in their lives.

It was, for most of them, a design wrought in faith and hope, two qualities which rarely bring their bearers to good ends. But for the remainder of the year the people at Rising Souls lived tolerably well on their pooled savings, plus those of the Teacher and what charity he'd acquired on the way. It was a treasury meant to last until the end of days.

It was in these flush times and on the grounds of Rising Souls that Isaac Patterson learned to walk, toddling on bowlegs back and forth between the clapping hands of sunburnt girls not much older than himself who were given charge of the small ones, learned to speak and sing and to lie still and flat on the ground long enough for the world to forget about him and resume its being. Learned to find good paths in the footprints of the older children when they went to cut rushes at the river's edge, dragging back the stalks for the women to weave the tall wicker seat where the Teacher would sit.

In another time the Teacher might have overseen a sheetmetal arena full of worshippers, might have seen his face mirrored in glowing screens tall as houses, but as it stood he towered from his chair on the porch overlooking the pool, reflected in the awed faces of the women and in the growing bellies of more than a few.

Among whom, it so happened, Isaac's mother was soon to be found.

Neda had seen the Teacher whispering to her before nightly lesson, and after dinner the girl had disappeared with him. In that moment, Neda hid herself from the idiot smiles of the other women, their muted cheer that the girl had been "chosen." That night Neda lay awake, waiting for the girl to come back, which she did not, having been taken into the Teacher's house officially, so Neda discovered the next morning at dawn prayer.

For weeks afterwards Neda couldn't catch the girl alone. She was always in the presence of the Teacher or the core group of other women, the chosen of the chosen. Even when Neda brought Isaac to her, hoping the child might stir something in her, the girl would only give the dreamy smile she, like all the rest but Neda, increasingly wore. Greeted the boy as you might a well-meaning stranger.

So Neda was startled and felt more than a small surge of hope when the girl came to her at the clothesline one dim evening between ablutions and dinner and said she was afraid. Neda let the sheet fall and took the girl's hands and asked her, softly, why. Hoping that whatever she said would be the beginning of their leaving here. But the hope died as soon as the girl opened her mouth.

She was afraid, the girl said, that the time of the birth would fall past the date of the end of the world. Maybe, she wondered, the child wouldn't even be one of the chosen and the girl would be bolted up to heaven in a beam of light only to find herself standing empty before God. (When she said this Neda imagined the light to be the color of the girl's eyes. An otherworldly green.) But then again, the girl went on, how wonderful a child born in Heaven would be. A child who never knew this world and all its hurts.

As she listened, hating herself, hating love, Neda realized that this whole time the girl's hands had never closed around her own.

As a girl on the island of her youth Neda would accompany her father into the groves of olive and carob where he strung belled nets to catch the flocks of turtledove and chaffinch that stopped there on their way across the sea, the island a lighting place for refugees as is ever the case.

If the moon was right you could round a bend in the path and suddenly see miles of hillsides in the shadow of the three-fingered mountain glittering with the eyes of the trapped. The birds would be cooked in enormous copper pans nested with garlic and raisins, their tender bones and the strong dark meat of their thumb-sized breasts said to grant virility to men who ate them. And as she grew older Neda wondered if the birds were to blame for the thoughts and wants that thrilled and troubled her. Those moments, when she would bite her lip and turn from the damp dressfront of a young wife washing clothes in the plaza fountain or while walking to the market fall behind to watch the sway of a cousin's hips, came unbidden and with mounting urgency. Eventually she stopped searching for an answer, her mind more occupied with survival. What being of such a nature taught you was that the world would never forgive you for it.

Now the birds came to her more and more. She looked around at the women and the gaunt sickly children of Rising Souls, and she thought of small things twitching in a net.

Three

A lean and bitter year, 1892.

While elsewhere electricity coursed for the first time through homes and lampposts and the bodies of criminals, the people at Rising Souls burned through the last of their kerosene before the end of the fall. Pine-knots and pitch in winter. When the revelation was near, and the Teacher retreated into his cottage with the girl and a few chosen, their accumulated stores were near depleted and their funds long gone. What crops they'd planted—white corn, sweet potatoes— couldn't support them. Neda led parties of them to claw oysters at low tide or into the woods to scratch with makeshift hoes for wild roots. And some snuck out to beg at the fishing camps, where the wives of fishermen away gave them sides of smoked mullet, Neda meanwhile learning paths and disused roads and cattle traces so that she could cover miles of ground in darkness. Finally the Teacher barred all such travel and intercourse, as he called it, with the outside. But Neda kept going until she was caught, having made the mistake of sharing her fish with a toothy girl from Alabama who, after she'd eaten her piece to the bone, went and told.

Next morning the Teacher had the women assemble before the cottage, and in the dawning light they whipped Neda's legs with green cane-stalks until she bled. The girl she loved, by now heavy-bellied like she'd been when they first met, tottered as she stooped and swung but didn't fail to draw blood.

Neda, eyes shut, raised her head to the sky.

Isaac too had taken to wandering at night. He would wake and slip from between the rickets-bent bodies of other children and pad out of the bunkhouse, walking until the soles of his feet were numb from the cold. Beneath his feet, in the ground, reptiles and frogs slept, their lives infinitesimally slowed. His own small life slowing with every passing day. On these nights he encountered whirring clouds of insects and the bats that broke like shards of the dark itself out of the night sky to feed on them. He often confused his waking life and dreams: The low, smooth movement of a shadow spilling down the bank of the creek, a panther come to drink; flicking the liver-colored cup of its tongue, the panther eyed him for a moment and then spilled back up the way it came. And it was on one such night that he saw or dreamed he saw the Teacher carrying something small and wrapped in cloth out to the little clearing in the woods behind the cottage. Saw or dreamed he saw the Teacher fall to his knees and set the bundle down and start digging in the dirt. Clawing with his big hands. From behind a screen of saw palmetto, Isaac watched the Teacher dig, heard his mumbled prayers and curses, until suddenly the man stood up and looked his way. Then Isaac was running, holding his breath all the way back to the bunkhouse. He wouldn't be caught, and the memory of this event would not survive in full. It would pass, like the dead half sister whose burial he'd witnessed, into other forms: a turtle floundering in a dry creekbed, a horse-trampled fox panting at the roadside, the memory of helpless things, a sadness he could not explain even when he had the words to do so.

That May they watched the river sink, the beginnings of a drought that would wither northwest Florida and lower Georgia on through summer. The air was dusty and tinged with the smoke of distant wildfires. Daylight chased the children into spots of shade, where they watched their mothers shuffle by. Legs like bones made visible by the light blazing through their thin shifts and dresses. Hauling buckets of water that grew lighter day by day. Hauling skeletal branches of wood. Hauling each other, growing light and bony themselves.

The first time Isaac drowned he was kneeling at the spring-fed pool, gulping the brassy water he knew it was forbidden to drink and that if anyone caught him he would be punished even as he retched it up. Then he was empty and drifting facedown in the pool, the fibers of his ragged clothes swelling thirstily as the water sucked him under.

Through the bubbles of his last breaths shot a desperate clawed hand that snatched him by the collar, wrenched him up. Out of the gray falling world and into the light. When he came to, he found himself caught in a fierce embrace; lights swam before his eyes and he couldn't see who held him, who clapped his back so that his chin jolted at their sharp shoulder.

Neda felt the sudden hitch in the boy's stomach and then the rush of water running down her back, warmed by its time inside him. Lately she'd been following the boy, carrying him now and then, watching, for she could no longer stand the sight of his mother. During the night of the dead child's birth, which was in fact the third day of labor, when one of the empty-eyed women who'd been midwifing came and asked her to help, Neda told the girl for the last time that she loved her. Whispered to her in her pain. Told her that her baby was dead. But there was nothing there in the girl's eyes. She might have said it to a stone. And so she'd left the girl and the dead child to the roomful of thin keening women, passing on the stairs the Teacher, whose face for the first time wore some hint that his control was waning, a glint of fear.

Now holding this child who she'd helped bring into the world and like all of them was dying, she knew what she would do. She held Isaac out at arm's length and studied him, how he favored his mother who no longer cared for him or for Neda, and, she admitted now, never had at all. The further we are from love, the more we see it remembered, traced, in the other things. She would take him, tonight or the night after. These green eyes blinking, the mouth that has air only because of you. She would go. Love had brought her there and, now, love would lead her out.

◆ ◆ ◆

Not long after the disappearance of Neda and the boy, the end came for Rising Souls. Brought on not by anyone's god, but by a team of workmen from Tallahassee who rode down the sand path in a pair of oxcarts loaded with tools and fresh pinewood caskets. The workmen had been hired by a group of Northeasterners to exhume the bodies of their loved ones who'd died there in its heyday as a convalescent home. These same families had other sons, uncles, fathers, buried in mass graves on battlefields and they would suffer no more of theirs to lie in Southern dirt. An agent had been sent ahead to confirm usufruct with the current owners of the land—apparently a Christian Home for Wayward Girls and Frail Women—but the agent had embarked instead on an epic whoring drunk on the company dime. When conscience and sobriety overtook him at the end of his weeklong spree, the agent forged the necessary papers and reported to the Northeasterners that all was well and the disinterment could proceed.

In the late morning the oxcarts passed through the last stand of stunted trees and halted, the teams grunting and stamping at the parched ground. The men shifted where they sat among the coffins, their excitement at seeing a place packed with easy women suddenly stolen, like their breath, as the flyblown stench enclosed them and they watched their foreman get down and make his way past the stilled outbuildings, heading toward the cottage.

—You smell that?

—Hoo lord.

—Maybe they already dug them boys up.

The foreman waited on the porch, knocking, calling out to the shuttered windows, before he finally nudged the unlatched door open and stepped inside. The workmen watched. For what seemed to them a long time everything was quiet, nothing moved. When the foreman reappeared, ash-gray and quaking, he stumbled out into the yard, where he sat on a stump with his head in his hands and couldn't, for all the good-natured questions of the men who came to his side, be persuaded to move or to say what he'd seen. The workmen left him with his thoughts, the image which would never leave him all the days of his life, and went into the cottage and the bunkhouses and saw for themselves. Soon the sound of them retching and their shouts of astonishment reached the foreman, who remained motionless on his stump as they came to join him in his daze. Few of the men who were there that day would know good sleep again.

Later the theory was put forward that some disease had swept through the place, but the bodies were so far gone that the cause of death was only determined months later by a coroner's inquest held at the capitol, the details of which (the depositions of the workmen and the coroner's report describing the suicide by poisoning of some four-teen persons) were quickly and quietly buried, with the ease available to men governing a state that had in recent memory been wild and who wanted nothing more than to show that it was a prime and fortunate place in the world.

Four

They were now many miles into the countryside, heading west. Three nights on the road, or what passed for a road, without encountering another soul. Neda had chosen their direction for the clouds she'd seen lowering on the day she'd saved Isaac from the pool. The promise of rain. She did not seek civilization or the company of people; that part of her had died in the desperation that made her finally abandon the only person she had ever loved. And more, she knew what the law of this country held in store for an unaccompanied woman with a child, much less a woman of her nature: these were the days when it was seen as fit to remove all the errant from our midst, the days of asylums, the days when a husband or some other man might, with a signature, consign an impudent wife to a five-by-eight cell for the rest of her life. Neda had spent some time in similar quarters, on charges of degeneracy, and sworn she never would again.

When they slept the boy would make a trap of himself, wedging his hands flat under her so that if Neda stirred in the night he would know and wake also. Feeling him there, or seeing him in full light in disintegrating clothes or sucking on a moonsnail shell, she would be overcome with loss and the cruel strangeness of it all, like someone who escapes their burning house with whatever object is at hand, watching her former life turn to ashes in the sky.

In the sawgrass plains that skirted the coast, she pulled sandspurs from Isaac's long brown hair and snapped stalks of aloe to rub into his skin and hers. When they came upon signs of habitation—smoke or tended roads—they began to travel at night. Dawn would find her thatching out a blind for them to sleep in, and as soon as Neda lay down, he'd be there, his hands wedged beneath where she was heaviest. He seldom spoke, but by the sixth day he'd begun to call her mama and she didn't have the heart to stop him.

They caught the rain on the afternoon of the eighth day, the sky burst, the ground suddenly rushing past their feet. As they came into a stretch of thick woods Neda fell to her knees and drank from where the roots of an oak formed a bowl. Isaac, watching, did the same.

The rain kept on and hid all sound, so Neda spoke her secrets and her rage. Things she'd told his mother and things she never could.

—You only let me touch you because you were tired and selfish. You never loved me and you never loved him. You were cruel. You were stupid.

The sky webbed with lightning as she lifted him to cross a swollen creek. Slipping in the slick clay of the disappearing bank, she gripped roots exposed by the flood and had to hold tightly to keep them both from being swept away.

—I was weak and worthless, but I loved you and that mattered.

They walked through the heart of the storm, the boy riding her back. Darkness fell and Neda knew she was climbing only by the pain in her thighs. The ache and burn fading as they reached the crest, then a blast of light stunned her and a great outrush of motion, something fast and enormous blowing by them in the dark.

Thrown backward, she curled, cupping Isaac's head as the ground around them trembled. At dawn the rain had cleared and Neda saw they had fallen beside some train tracks. Not six inches from the ties. She stood and helped the boy to stand, and they saw spread out before them clear-cut woods, the stumps of yellow and longleaf pine pocking the land from the other side of the train tracks to the horizon, where only a low, dark line held the promise of cover.

In Isaac's memory, all of this was changed. The teachers at the West Florida Baptist Boys' Home where he would live from the age of two to six would urge him to recall his early childhood as steeped in the sin of another, something that was only overcome and ended by the good graces of the Lord. His mother was an unsaved sinner who'd abandoned him after putting him through a short stint of earthly hell, and he was lucky to be where he was.

But there were moments that returned to him. Trees towering and then no trees at all. Waves of heat and the baked body of a dead thing in the grass. Thirst. Lying on the ground, feeling the warm dirt against his belly, drinking dirty water from a pond; the ground a deep burnt orange veined with gray clay and wisps of white sand, a place where the water is the color of the ground.

It must be said that the Baptists were doing what they thought best, but the same theology that urged them to acts of uncommon charity also insisted that behind each life was a sin-steeped story ending in either redemption or damnation—most often, the latter. So his story, his life and hers with it, would be made to fit the frame.

As it happened, Neda had drunk first from the clay pit and only when she'd judged it vile but not poisonous had she prodded him to do the same, turning from the sight of a child having to drink like a dog.

The sound of her choking and the sight of her tears did not survive, only the color. An aura marking time. Not her strong hands carrying him and parting branches from their way, not her voice, not her sorrow, not her love.

In his dreams there is a woman and she lifts him above the flood. Her hair is long and black-red, and she ties it with blades of sawgrass so that she seems to come out of the earth. Out of the woods they travel. She holds his hand and pulls him and there is always some danger to escape; she is always frightened. She lifts him from the baking ground the color of the water he's choked down and wipes his face with the inside of her wrist. She is not his mother, but something more. And she would exist in the secret place beyond the teachers and their god and the sins they had invented for her. In him, among the animals. Safe from what memory and men would have.

Five

Three hunters and as many hounds pursued them in the woods west of Round Lake. The hunters were on horseback and had been afield for half the night in search of coons but now had a mind for other sport. They rode and whooped, drunk enough to be both ardent and confused, even on a cloudless night. The moon high, the woods silvered and unreal.

She ran through this nightmare country with Isaac on her back, panting up the hills and thrashing through the tangled growth. She hid with him in foxdens ripe with urine and in the boughs of trees. And when she would judge the hunters far enough away and she would quit whatever hidingplace she'd found, the hunters would by fool luck stumble on their trail again. She ran on, hearing in the distance the hunters' laughter and cries that were meant to mimic that of the Indians their forefathers had driven out.

Dropped alone in that stretch of pinewoods stood Bill's Wine-shop, a tavern for railmen of the F.C.&P. line. At that hour, past two in the morning, an engineer from Georgia swayed pissing from the back porch. A mist had crept over the open ground between the tavern and the trees, and through it burst a woman with a small child padlocked around her neck. The Georgia engineer watched her race out of the mist and past the tavern, over the rail lines and into the next stand of trees. When the hunters rode cursing into the yard, their blown horses jostling to the trough, he was standing in the same place, staring at the woods into which she'd disappeared and shaking his head at how strange life was. Seeing the hunters, the Georgian called out to his fellows at the bar, who soon appeared on the porch righteous and armed with wrenches and axehandles thwacking in their hard hands. Only one hunter managed to escape the fight that followed, but he would be enough.

Neda heard the gunfire and screams and hurried deeper into the woods, sliding downhill to the moonlit mirror of a lake, and skirting this came into a region of rushing creeks and the sound of deeper waters falling. In a clearing she stopped before the ruins of a grist mill that had supplied soldiers of the late war. Stripped of wood and rope, the fulcrum cast off into the bushes, the millstones lay gray and massive like overturned megaliths, shoots of bamboo growing through their bores. She fell behind the millstones, gasping, and eased Isaac down into the wedge between the surfaces of cold granite flecked with quartz that sparkled in the moonlight, where he sat wrenching at his wrists like a man released from shackles, eyes wide and searching.

—Stay, she said, then went quiet, listening.

But Isaac tried to crawl out, the hands of the woman he would remember as his mother forcing him deeper into the gap until he was stuck there like a seed between the millstones. He heard the horse and hunter coming on and was overcome with horror when Neda bolted up and scrambled out of sight.

He was suddenly alone, and what can be said of such a moment and the fear he felt except that it was terrible and total. Isaac shut his eyes and imagined himself in a den of warm animals, watched over by beings greater than himself, as the sounds of running and shouts and the thundering horse grew distant for a time, so he could almost believe that everything was better, and then the night exploded into screams.

For the pounding of her blood and breath, Neda hadn't heard the roar of the waterfall until she'd almost gone over the rim. Pitched forward by her own momentum, she clawed at the limbs and roots that grew there, catching herself at the last moment on a sapling's stubborn trunk. She hung there as leaves blown by her progress drifted on currents of air into the mouth of the tight stone chute whose bottom she couldn't see, and she had just begun to pull herself up when horse and hunter plunged over the side, and were suspended for an unreal instant in the open air, a tangle of rein and man and mane, before dropping out of sight. Though not of sound. It takes a long time for men and horses to die of shattered bones.

Isaac in the space between the stones, afraid to open his eyes. Trying to stop hearing what he heard. But then there she was, kneeling at the gap, all cut and bloody but whole and here and saying to come out. *It's all right now.*

◆ ◆ ◆

They traveled on ridges of dry ground, out of the marsh and saltmeadow to the dunes and the shore of the sea. Oleander and sea oat in thick patches; white sprays of spurge nettle in bloom. She knew none of these things—the landscape had outpaced all her grasp, her youth of rock beaches and cliffs.

Their torn, blackened feet stirred hot clouds of sugar sand. Neda awed at the whiteness of this termination and the sudden explosion, when they climbed the last dunes, of the Gulf.

Numberless shorebirds adrift above waves and strutting stiff-legged in the break. Mullet shot like jets of mercury from the water. She wavered there, waiting for an answer. She'd come so far wanting to escape loss and pain and others, and now she knew there was nothing left to do but keep moving. So they did, down the beach and to the east, where parties of terns and black-bellied plovers and sundowners raced ahead of them.

They crossed unknowingly the tight neck of land that connected the continent to the island which had yet to receive an Anglo-Saxon name that stuck. On the beach, the wet sand breathed, sputtering with clams, and in the clear breaking waves to the left of Neda and Isaac schools of bull minnow and snapper fry were shadowed by small sharks. Families of dolphins breaching in strong, smooth arcs swam parallel to their course.

At the point where the island jutted out into the bay, the sun's glare was so great that she could see nothing and she laid a hand to Isaac's head, still hoping for some answer but knowing now that none would come. Only faceless voices and the sun burning them away. She thought this would be where they would die, burnt up, and they might drift as ashes out over the water. Then the voices came again.

—Miss?

—Excuse me, *miss*?

Neda turned, squinting for the glare, and saw them. On the other side of the point, on a broad flowered quilt, sat women in straw hats and fluttering ribbons and clothes as white as the sand. The one who spoke stood above the bursting stars of their parasols while another took a nervous bite of a white triangle she held in one gloved hand. Neda felt herself slipping as the woman approached, speaking in a crystal voice.

—Miss, are you all right?

Six

Floating in a soap bubble. That was how he would remember it. Lifted up and suspended in some soft, shining element, the air thick with ointments and colognes and the sharp tang of borax in the bedsheets when he woke. The strangeness of light filtered through perfect windowpanes and curtains thin as mist.

He lay alone in the bed in the turret of the summer people's house and waited for Neda to come. He guessed she was being kept in some other room, but the only voices that came drifting up to him were those of the vacationers, a Pennsylvania coal heiress and her daughters. He heard footsteps on the stairs and in the evenings a piano being played. He'd never known the sound before and when the youngest daughter came to check on him she found him weeping, frozen, in the bed.

They kept him for a month and a half. Fed him on lemonade and bowls of beef broth whose surface shuddered with beads of fat. Then rice puddings, then fish. It was the era of faddish philanthropy and foundlings were in vogue, the popular literature of the day rife with charity. The heiress and her daughters sent for clothes, cut Isaac's long hair, and with the cold discretion available to the rich, they gently fended off all his questions about the woman he called his mother as the heiress made entreaties to the few orphan asylums in the state of Florida.

Neda could see that the rich girls were suspicious, like their mother, taking account of Neda's features and trying to make them fit those of the boy. For the four days she spent at the house, Neda turned herself to stone, taking food and water but giving nothing back. She responded to none of their questions, and when, on the fifth day, the sheriff of Washington County came to collect her, her silence was unbroken and would have remained so had the youngest daughter, a doughy girl called Amelia, not run up to her as she was being led out, saying,

—Don't you even want to see him? Won't you at least tell him goodbye?

Standing beside the sheriff, who smelled of lather and gun oil, Neda stared resigned at the girl whose cast-off dress she wore.

The girl summoning all her pomp:

—Well won't you?

—And what good will that do, Neda said. Who will it help sleep?

Stunned, Amelia couldn't summon a response, and when, later in life, this speechless moment would return to trouble her, she would remember how the dark woman shook her head and let herself be led away, uncaring, as unfortunate persons often are, always complicit in their own sorrows.

Neda was brought to the sheriff's house rather than the jail itself. The sheriff, whose name was Rayburn, was only slightly older than his jurisdiction, having come down from Baltimore with frontier dreams and an aged aunt who acted as housekeeper though they had been lovers since his youth. Neda was given a room across from the aunt, and the two of them spent their days in silent housework, cooking the sheriff's meals and listening to him talk through dinner.

For five years Rayburn had enjoyed a peaceable county, where whatever crimes occurred did so without his knowledge, for the most part. Until now, and there was the matter of this woman and the dead man at the bottom of the falls and the other at Bill's Wineshop. That particular corpse had fallen, by chance, in the next county, whose cracker sheriff would no doubt find this woman and her trail of calamity of interest. But the sheriff noticed that his aunt was somewhat perked by Neda's presence, and so he decided, confiding in no one, that he would say nothing of her or the boy at the vacationers' house. Handing her over did not appeal to his tailored-buckskin sense of gallantry and, besides, no one knew for certain whether she had done anything at all other than be mad, which to his eyes she surely was.

The days passed and the aunt and Neda kept their silence as they scrubbed and cooked and shook flakes of alum on the floor, even as the aunt saw her stealing bits of things to hide beneath her bed—a knife, pins, washcloths, a pan—and, as autumn neared, food. And when one midnight in late September the sheriff was called away to attend the burning of a house, Neda readied to leave. She made no special effort for stealth, and hearing her the aunt sat up awake, watching the dark gap of her door, which she left ajar for her nephew. The aunt couldn't see beyond the doorway but felt just the same that Neda was there. And, because she was a bit dreamy and melancholy by nature, the aunt spoke a line of poetry in misremembered schoolgirl Greek, about another such soul who traveled like the night.

For the first time in the aunt's memory, she heard the woman laugh.

—That's a very old way of saying it, Neda said.

The aunt in her rumpled nightclothes felt the sum of her life, whose consolations were few beyond the touches of the boy she'd ruined into an early maturity, settle grimly on her bent back. When she spoke again her voice was hoarse.

—It's all old, the aunt said. Everything. There's nothing between the then and the now.

The aunt stared at the gap in the door, not expecting an answer nor even fully understanding what she'd meant, and all that came to her were the footsteps going out and soon even these were gone.

There are those who condescend to tell you about love and loss, and have known neither at its full pitch, which is nearest to madness and sends us out to wander unknown, night-black countries, seeking what we cannot have, the land growing less and less familiar with each step.

Neda, twenty-three years old and heading down the road, in possession of little more than her life. But this would be enough.

◆ ◆ ◆

When the suit between the families of the northern convalescents and the contractor was settled in a Florida court, whose deliberations were belabored by the appearance of a sordid woman in a feathered hat who claimed to be (and was) the wife of Newell James Brose Jr., also known as "the Teacher," three years had passed since anyone had set foot on the grounds of Rising Souls. And because the first workmen had for the most part drifted elsewhere, and what few remained either refused to return or had so poisoned other teamsters with what they'd seen, the men who were engaged to do the digging had to be got from as far as Georgia and Alabama. They came in wagons loaded with coffins and tools, in the fall of 1895, and found the outbuildings overgrown by creeper vines and the spring choked with a kind of waterlily none of them recognized. Only the cottage was untouched. Flaking paint and a few shingles missing; on its porch a wicker chair blown down by the wind.

These men were not so different from the ones who'd gone before. You'd be hard-pressed to distinguish between them in, say, a photograph of a crowd jostling beneath the burnt, twisted body of a black man, which for most would be the only time their pictures were ever taken. But they were single-minded and hungry, and before sundown they would dig up twenty-three bodies, pry them from their rotted coffins and shovel them into the new ones bound for little towns on the Eastern Seaboard. When it happened that one man's shovel turned up the skeleton of an infant wrapped in a kitchen rag, none paused. The man tilted the contents of his shovel onto the dirt piled beside the grave, and when they exhumed its nominal occupant, a young consumptive from Tewksbury, Massachusetts, and placed him in his new home, the man scooped the infant up and poured it in. The small bones and hollow skull lay across the chest of the dead young man, whose folded arms and gaping mouth seemed to refuse its company. Then the coffin was nailed shut, marked with the name from the headstone, and like the others hauled out to the depot, where the stationmaster stamped them as freight.

In a well-kept plot hard by a home for the insane, child and man would wait out eternity, presided over by mourners who aged and died and were themselves buried and mourned by another generation ignorant of the small interloper in their family ground. And like them, we might think our lives to be distinct, though the distinction exists only in so far as we are there to perceive it. Lives, like the bones which briefly hold them, are all related and who can say where one ends and another begins.

PART 2

The Light that Came from Beside the Sea

1896 – 1909

One

We come from this: the Gulf, the sea of storms. A place of generation and memory, for here all forms may be found antecedent to one another: the current is remembered in the sands it shapes, and hurricanes in their vast movements over the face of the waters whirl as do bodies of stars in the infinite dark. All our endings and beginnings, here, in the forms of life igniting and extinguishing.

Sixty-six million years ago, in the night, at the southwestern edge of the Gulf, a sky-long bow of fire ending in a second sun arced over the earth, and struck. Onshore stones were blasted into sand and the sand boiled into liquid for an instant and then turned to glass as over the water rose a dome of viscous light around which billowed the vaporized sea, taller than the peaks of distant mountains, hurtling past the clouds. For months thereafter frantic lifeforms scrambled beneath a sky ribboned with new and terrible colors. Then came hissing, burning rains and the fall of ash and darkness. The shadow in which hitherto insignificant, furred creatures with warm bodies and quick hearts would become, among other things, human.

Much later, to the north and east, the mountains lost their ice. A ten-thousand-year spell coming to an end. Rivers of melt veined with sediment, numberless grains of limestone, granite, quartz traveled south to the end of the continent and fanned out from the mouths of rivers and accrued in the shallows of the sea. Meeting currents and the fragments of shell and bone they brought, the sediments formed the barrier islands that stretched from the great curve of what we know as Florida to the seat of life, the Yucatán. There the descendants of the beings whose cradle had been ash and shadow built vast coastal temples overlooking the sea where, long ago, the stone had struck. The descendants prospered there, and when it came time to give a name to creation they called it *the light that came from beside the sea.*

◆ ◆ ◆

Cold bleeding out as possibility gathers in smoke and mist. The declines of glaciers and civilizations are not so different from the course of a single life.

When Mrs. Patterson collected him from the Baptist Boys' Home, Isaac carried all he owned in a paper-wrapped bundle tied with string. He was six years old. Boarding the westbound train for Mississippi, a porter tried to help him with the bundle, but Isaac yanked back and stared at the man, furious. Mrs. Patterson, apologizing, put a hand to the child's shoulder and eased him from the platform up the foliated iron steps, hoping this was not a terrible mistake.

She was forty-six years old and of a liberal bent. Her husband had retired early from business, bringing her and their two sons from New Orleans to the coast of Mississippi and a town called Maurepas on the eastern shore of Biloxi Bay, and their relationship was uncommonly warm. From the early days of their marriage, they would rendezvous during his workday for covert bouts of lovemaking. As a younger woman she'd gotten him fired from one job for the frequency of these noonday departures and had horrified his parents when a note from her was found that, as Mr. Patterson's father had said, would have stunned a whore. Now on occasion she still found herself, at midday, burning up, and she was proud that her body and her drives had yet to fail her, though the possibility of bearing children had passed. When on vacation in St. Augustine Mrs. Patterson had decided that she wanted to take on another child, there was no argument.

Stepping onto their car, she found their seats and gently persuaded Isaac to part with his things. A flash then of normalcy, the boy nodding meekly and taking his seat while she stowed the bundle away. Her only regret in that moment was that her husband would not be there to meet them at the station in Biloxi. It was November and the ducks were thick over the marshes to the west, where he kept a small hunting camp in the Rigolets in Louisiana. He was far from unfeeling but was often in his own world, one governed by migrations and spawns, and they'd arranged for their sons, Ben, the youngest, and David, seventeen, to have some time with him before she and Isaac arrived. By now he'd be crouching in the blind with Ben and David and the birddog Lu, holding the oil-cloth-wrapped Italian birding gun, a gift from Sicilian friends. Her husband had made his money in real estate, buying lots and decaying houses in the French Quarter from retreating Creoles and selling them to the most recent wave of immigrants, from Italy. And because he did so fairly and treated people well, there were many who considered themselves in his debt. Thus the shotgun fit for a duke and the crates of oranges and shoeboxes of *cuccidati* on their doorsteps each Christmas. They called him Mister Pat and when, in 1890, eleven Italian men had been lynched, he was one of the few who'd spoken against it. She considered this as the train shook and vented steam, the gifts, their lives and the beauty with which they shielded themselves from the world.

The boy, Isaac, fidgeting and silent, had no doubt seen and been touched by the ugliness of this world. Of course, the heavy women and soft-voiced men of the Boys' Home had assured her that Isaac was young enough and gentle and would do God and family proud. (Most of the other boys would be adopted by childless farm couples in need of backs, or not at all. These were the days of surplus children, orphan trains chugging down from the cities of the East, seeding the inland states with parentless youth.) Mrs. Patterson bore little love for God, and having given him one child of hers already (a girl, two, fever) considered that grim transaction the end of their relationship. Still, she could be swayed by the spiritual as much as the rational, and read the Kabbalists and the agnostic Ingersoll with equal interest. She was an early proponent of sunbathing, and thus the cause of several minor scandals in her small town on the Mississippi coast. Her true love, though, was for filling life as fully as she could with beauty, for herself, her husband, her children, and now, she hoped, this young boy whose small shoulders jerked at the shriek of the brakes.

Now on the train with him seated opposite, Mrs. Patterson saw that he was not the feral thing of her deepest fears. Almost as soon as the train bucked into motion, she saw the change in him that wasn't a change at all, but the slow unveiling of who he was. Beneath the sweep of brown hair his eyes grew bright and he spoke, chattered as though he'd been waiting for a listener, and before they were out of Jackson County she was thoroughly charmed. He asked her where they were going and she talked about the house on the sound and the islands and the sea beyond that. She told him how certain fish swam in hoards to the beach and how on summer nights ghost crabs swarmed and at spring moons others shaped like bowls with swords for tails beached themselves to mate.

—And when their eggs hatch, she said, what's left behind is a coin-purse for mermaids.

He nodded gravely at this, then asked what a mermaid was. Mrs. Patterson explained as best she could, and again he was nodding.

—Like angels in the sea?

—Something like that. They used to do mischief to sailors, but not anymore.

The train car rocked, hurtling through pine forest.

—But are they real like angels?

—*Well*, she began, but decided on another tack.

In her handbag she'd brought along a framed photograph of them all, taken last May. She took the picture out and, handing it to Isaac, told him who each person was. The light that came streaming in as the train entered open ground and hugged the sea caught the gilt frame so that it glowed in his hands. For a long time Isaac studied the picture, and she listened, learning his voice—the light twang of the accent he would lose in the coming years as he adopted her own—watching happiness wash over him as he gave the names out like a prayer.

—Mother. Father. David. Ben.

She touched his hand, just barely.

—And now you, she said.

Two

He was the youngest by six years and fell gamely into the slipstream of the Patterson boys. Within a week of their return Isaac could be seen trailing them close, just as twelve-year-old Ben went in the steps of the older David, playing understudy to their nested roles with an outsized eagerness that bled over into everything he did, just gulping up the world. They rowed with Isaac at the bow of their skiff, where he jostled happily for a place beside the dog, Lu, leaning against her thick furred ribs as they went through the calm waters of the sound and into the marshes for solitary bull redfish near troughs and at the feet of oysterbeds.

Not to say his coming to the family was without difficulty. Isaac suffered from bouts of fear at random and for the first few days wouldn't leave Mrs. Patterson's side, so she slept on a trundle cot beside his bed until he could be persuaded to share a room with Ben. He ate late and in secret, balled up fistfuls of white bread to chew alone in his room, which troubled her much less than what she saw as his almost frightening need for affection and, worse, his willingness to accept it from any and everyone who would give it. He had none of the reticence typical of little boys. Set him on a bench with a woman he'd been introduced to ten seconds prior, a friend of hers in town perhaps, or at the Florida Water–scented counter of the dress shop, and you would find him soon enough with some cooing lady running fingers through his hair. And seeing how utterly pleased he was and how he crowded happily into the chests of women, she knew that he would be trouble later in life and was not surprised when, at fourteen, he was compromised by the much-older sister of a classmate. Which escapade earned him a good-sized scar on his back from when the girl's outraged mother discovered them behind a garden shed and pitched a flowerpot at him. He was never a rake, never unkind, and she was glad for this but he was so eager for everything he could get in terms of affection that Mrs. Patterson worried that it would be his downfall. With time Isaac's fear would lessen, but the habit of eating and the mania for affection would stay with him all his life. But at least, she thought, he did not flinch or fear being beaten, which spoke well for the Baptists, though for a while he was concerned that the rest of the Pattersons were going to Hell and that he would be left alone again and this time forever.

In the winter Mrs. Patterson herded Isaac and Ben into what had once been a barn, now swept of hay and converted into a studio and patrolled by a scabby Manx called Wildman. There she intended for her youngest boys, sufficiently tired, to cultivate themselves (and if this happened to grant her time alone with her husband around midday, then all the better). All around were scattered the detritus of David's fleeting interests. A table of leatherwork and chisels set beside a potter's kickwheel, long dry; above it were shelves of jarred chemicals and specimens of David's taxidermy, which he'd pursued after learning that it had been Theodore Roosevelt's hobby as a youth, just as he'd taken up football and would later enlist in the army for the war in Cuba. So Isaac learned how to lay ropes of clay and shape a bowl, how to skin birds and carve wood. Mrs. Patterson watched, delighted at this reignited childhood.

More than anything Isaac was mad for drawing, for colors. Even at some other task, his hand would wander to a pencil and a scrap of paper and he was drawing everything. Mrs. Patterson would keep this especially in her heart, that she'd been the one who gave him the passion of his life, loving this in the way the love of the openhearted is really a mirror for the joy of those around them. How he took to the pens and paints and crayons, and soon the studio was filled with bolts of canvas (much too good for a child) and the wood for frames. They found him a stool and he would perch there for hours, hunched over a table or craning over the corner of a pad, filling space with what he'd seen throughout the day and many things he never had. Darting fish and crouched cats mingled among elephants and winged horses, all of which she'd add to her menagerie of treasures made by the other children.

But most of all she loved to wash his hands in the white enamel basin in the yard, working the pump and watching him dance for the chill of the gushing water. Loved the feel of his small fingers as they lost their smears of paint and charcoal. Sunsets and storms of colors, swirling, fading in the flow.

When spring came and it was warm enough the brothers taught Isaac to swim. It was painstaking work. First they sheltered him in a span of water no wider than their shoulders, corralled by their arms as he paddled, kicked, and spat. Then they made him travel back and forth between them, giving him a little more distance each day. He had to learn to stop looking up, searching bleary-eyed for them; to trust that they wouldn't go away. All of this was overseen by Lu, who, as a younger dog, had been known to dive in and retrieve the brothers with the gentle mouth of a mother, and now in the last year of her life could only sit and stare. And if Mrs. Patterson was ever worried that bringing Isaac into their lives was unkind to her natural children (a phrase she hated), she could look out from the porch and see David wading chest-deep, Ben up to his freckled collar bone, both slapping the sunlit water and urging Isaac on. But there was also a part of her that knew she was witnessing their lives in microcosm, the brothers drifting further apart each day, and Isaac, when you could see him at all, so focused on his own struggle that he might have been alone. At such times she had to stop herself from bolting up and hollering for them to stay close by, as she did one blustery day in June, seeing storm clouds gathering in the west. She found herself standing at the edge of the porch, fear like a stranger in her voice. Ben and David turning, waving to her, but Isaac churning on, oblivious, until David snagged him and held him up to her like a trophy. Isaac grinned, dripping, waved, and called out for her to watch, watch, watch, as he flipped from David's arms into the water.

There were no great storms that summer. The coast of Mississippi, a marshy toe extended out into the Gulf from the bloated body of the state, went unharmed. Biloxi did catch fire one night, and the Pattersons watched from their back porch as the sparks rose and the city on the western shore of the sound glowed like a coal. But the fire was contained, no lives lost. The days passed and the boys spread wider apart. By September Isaac could swim without pause the quarter mile across the narrow sound between their shore and Deer Island.

Three

Farther out lay the islands formed by glacial melts and sustained by sediments which in those days still flowed unimpeded from the river deltas. A few, the largest, were inhabited year-round by lighthouse keepers or small garrisons of bored soldiers, but most were no larger than suburban backyards, rising and falling with the tides. And there were reports, from the Choctaw and the Pascagoula before them, of an island that rose once every ninety years, remaining above the surface long enough to show faintly in the charts of a few early European expeditions and in the memories of grandparents. In the years to come a New Orleans speculator would build a casino on one of these capricious strands, betting not only against time and tide but that the precarious nature of the place itself was an attraction. (The casino Isle of Caprice would sink, along with one bartender and several members of a jazz band, in a storm at the end of 1928.) But back toward the shore, in the Mississippi Sound, Deer Island sat facing the mainland it had once been a part of, pared by storms in the previous century, and retained a few oaks and a stand of pines along its back. The island was owned in total by a New Orleans family called the Woolsacks, whose money was said to be in shipping, and it was occupied many summers by the wife and her two young children, a puny boy with blood-red hair and a girl you might politely call sturdy, whose own hair was somewhere between sunset and gold. There was another, older son who came with his father sometimes, but you might not see either for years. Those who did see them, father and son in cream-colored suits, would remark that they were alike in build (tending to lankness and not much height) and in the jut of their noses and chins, in the storm-green glares they shot from under the brims of their hats, in everything but name (the father's was Joseph and the oldest son's Angel) and age and most of all in voice: the father's French-tinged but bottoming out in a gravelly drawl while the son's had a lightness some guessed must've come from his mother and which worried certain men in a way they struggled to explain. Regardless, whatever these two said to your casual greeting or ill-chosen platitude, you knew they were not, as it were, nice people. The wife and mother was not much better regarded, though she had, in the year before Isaac came, invited a few locals to their newly completed home on the island. It was a grand house, high ceilings beamed with cedar, tall doors open to the beach fronted with yucca, which others called Spanish bayonet. The afternoon was, by all accounts, disastrous, though this didn't seem to bother Mrs. Woolsack, who introduced herself as Marina. She was taller and fairer-haired than the others and owned an un-American coldness. When they were shown in, the guests noted that she hadn't bothered to move her many piles of books. Her husband's people, she said, were from New Orleans, but she'd come from Cuba. And when one visitor, a judge, spoke brightly of Cuba's future as an American possession, she clicked her tongue and said something that made him blush. She sat with her guests on the veranda drinking chilled Ojen and never so much as winced at the havoc of her youngest children, a pair of terrors, a girl called Kemper and a boy named George but called Red. When they were home again, Mr. Patterson joked that the boy must've been named for the poet's line, "red in tooth and claw." The joke becoming far less funny when, a few weeks later, Mr. Patterson, talking to a friend who still lived in New Orleans, learned a bit more about the father, Joseph Woolsack, and his business, which details Mr. Patterson kept to himself except to say they weren't good.

For a long time that visit was the last of all but the most cursory dealings anyone had with the people on Deer Island. From the shore you could see the lights in the high windows, and passing fishermen notched sightings of the lady on the veranda, facing the sea with a book in her lap, face veiled by her hair, while her children squabbled in the surf.

When Isaac was able to swim to the eastern end of the island, the two youngest Woolsack children would sometimes lie in wait in the tall patches of bay cedar and then leap out and pelt him with shells until David or Ben chased them back. It was all near enough for Mrs. Patterson to see clearly: the red-haired boy streaking over the dunes, fists pumping; the girl, Kemper, a bright clot of danger stark against the sand, standing firm until the Patterson boys had gone back into the water. On his rare visits, the husband would prowl the island with a pistol and, together with his eldest son, hunt whatever they could find, delighting in the sounds of gunfire for their own sake, the youngest boy weaving between them like an ill-trained birddog.

So for a few weeks each year the Woolsacks existed parallel to the world, betraying no interest in their neighbors. To Mrs. Patterson, the wife was an object of pity, for her solitude and coldness, her absence from her husband. More than anything Mrs. Patterson felt that love was something you spent freely, and in all directions that you could, and that if everyone did so the world would be a finer place. She guessed, somewhat correctly, that for this woman and her family love was an entangled thing, tight as briars. Guessed also, edging closer to the truth, that the Woolsacks were better suited to the world as it was not the world of feelings. And yet there were times when she'd think of the woman as a kind of friend, a ghost haunting no one but herself.

In July of '98, when David was killed in the fighting at Daiquirí, Marina Woolsack sent her a short letter of condolence, quoting Shakespeare. Mrs. Patterson was so amazed by this and stunned already in her grief that she wrote back the very next day, thanking her. She never received a reply.

Four

Now it must be said who the Woolsacks were. They were the kind of people whom much can be said of, but little for. And if anything could be said in their favor, to make them graspable to those who consider themselves *good people*, the Woolsacks were honest, if only among themselves. The gnarled nature of their line and what sustained their lives was always kept in plain sight of the whole family, kept by the father and mother who'd perpetuated it, by the sons whose lives it would maul, and by the daughter, Kemper, who for all her life would struggle to understand them all. Families are machines of perpetual motion, forever fueled by one thing or another. (Myth. Pride. Expectation. Hope.) And even as a child Kemper knew the Woolsacks were a machine that ran on misery.

The foundation of their wealth, the girl knew, had been laid at the turn of the nineteenth century when her paternal grandfather, the first Angel Woolsack, a laypreacher, shifted his commerce from souls to the vessels that held them. Namely black bodies. He played no direct role, this ancestor she'd never known, owned no pens or auction-houses (though he did own several human beings) but became in short order a commodity speculator. Before that he'd supplemented his itinerant preaching with a series of failed ventures—stores, farms, revolutions— playing a small enough part in the United States acquisition of Louisi- ana and West Florida to loiter just at the margins of what we call history. But in the family his legacy was much discussed, one of those things they kept out in the light. A light the first Angel Woolsack had set him- self, for this grandfather had left a written account of his brutal youth and rise before blowing out his brains on the day New Orleans fell to Union troops in 1862. The stained and fragile manuscript, titled *Blood of Heaven*, was a wonder to Red, who read it avidly from the moment his father allowed it out of his locked desk. He pored over its pages and, growing up, would make games of the events in the book, and Kemper would play her part, as sisters must. When she read it, Kemper found no thrill in the actions of this terrifying being. Her grandfather had (as many do) returned to his fierce brand of religion just before his decline, and so the book had a mad jeremiadic tone, and even if you managed to drive this from your mind there was the fleshed prophecy of suicide waiting there for you, looming in the offing of heredity. Still, the book remained an object of reverence for father and sons. In this and many other ways, her mother's past and people were diminished. They were not beings of prophecy, a people with a Book.

Her mother had been orphaned as a girl in the wreck of a blockade- runner from Havana to New Orleans, and had charmed the command- ing general of the very American forces that had driven her parents' ship into the storm. She had been given a book of Shakespeare by the same commanding general's wife shortly after her rescue at sea. A twelve-year- old girl escorted via gunboat to the rebel mainland. A twelve-year-old girl, who was then abandoned by her last surviving relative, an uncle in New Orleans, to the care of his mistress, a free woman of color and neighbor of the Woolsacks. A girl who had survived in a place that didn't want her, with a people not her own, and, Kemper thought, after so much surviving had given up and married the boy at whose side she'd spent her every waking moment from the age of twelve.

Her mother was even more circumspect about her ancestors, Prussians who had come to oversee the construction of the Camagüey rail line, a people who'd chosen to remain in an alien country and then to forfeit their lives by leaving it. Kemper gathered what pieces she could of her mother's past those summers on Deer Island, and at other times. And, in one of those paradoxes that knot the hearts of daughters, she believed both that her mother's life was extraordinary as any hellfire preacher's and that her mother's resulting silence, her willingness to let her life be knocked aside by the crazed onward movement of the Woolsacks' grisly history, was cowardice or worse. Something like a suicide itself. So she grew to envy her oldest brother, who could leave them all on his journeys to Central America, where he oversaw the family's business in shipping and especially fruit—a sweetness that required no end of bloodshed—and she fought with her father, her mother, her brother, Red, her family, which meant of course that she was fighting herself.

Five

Mrs. Patterson kept Isaac home the fall after David's death, close to her and to Ben, who'd only just begun to gain his footing as the eldest at home when the news came. The officer's curt letter was followed one week later by the body of her firstborn, which they buried in the back beneath the big magnolia and a fine granite headstone. But in the spring, at her husband's urging, she surrendered the boy to school.

The schoolteacher was a young woman from Clinton, come to replace the last one, who'd died that December of diphtheria. New to the town and to teaching, on the first day she had her students write what she called their autobiographies. Little essays, only a page. The new teacher had a large, soft mouth, the habit of wringing her wrists, and believed children should only be beaten when absolutely necessary. At the end of the schoolday, she sat at her desk and read the essays, marking penmanship and spelling, learning what she'd have to teach.

She came to Isaac's formbook, the margins of his first pages already filled with drawings. After a few glazed moments noting the obvious (poor handwriting, middling spelling) her pencil stopped and she had to make herself read again what he'd written:

My first mother they said totchered me. She hurt me with her ways. We didnt have a house. We were barefoot on the road. We got chased. We had to live out in the woods and drank water from a dich. It was murke.

The young schoolteacher from Clinton, who'd seen and known some hardship, felt a small, soft pressure in her chest growing more urgent as she came to the end:

Now I have a real mother and a father and two brothers. One is dead. His name was David and he taut me how to swim. We live together in one place and I can have my favorite things. Im happy now and I will be happy for the rest of my life.

Which was true, the hope of it. And of all the times of his life, save maybe the first years of his marriage, his boyhood on the coast was the happiest.

When he was older, his teachers in art would say to forget what he knew. Begin again with the most basic forms. The line, the brushstroke. Your mind and heart and body all moving through your hand, and through your hand the stroke that makes the line. Tell him to seek some primal image or pigment, a definite beginning, to find the root of his work.

Color has an order, where memory has none. Color must be balanced thus:

Red

Purple-red   Red-orange

Purple   Orange

Blue-purple   Orange-yellow

Blue   Yellow

Green-blue   Yellow-green

Green

But memory cannot, and his childhood would come to him in rushes: His hand doubled by his father's, hauling up a net of crabs over the rail of a salt-gnawed footbridge. Rising through the water, the netted crabs change color, the brilliant blue about their claws and sides when they came up into the light of where we live. The *thwap* of sails and the shudder of the tiller in his hand, steering a boat for the first time. Island rookeries of bittern, blue peter, gallinule. Hold the speckled egg to the lamplight in a darkened room and see the dark splotches over the red world of the embryo. Nests of reed and sawgrass. A castoff fledgling peppered with ants and blinking. His father says to do nothing, but Isaac cups the tiny bird and goes to the shore and washes it in the water, then returns it to the nest where the squawking mother kicks it out again. He has seen his own mother wrap ducklings in a rag and tuck them in the front of her dress for warmth and the soothe of the beat of her heart. So he does this with the chick, which dies after a few minutes, regardless of his heart, and he learns what this means. Another dawn and he follows a formation of ducks with his shotgun, knocks two out of the sky, and learns again. In open, wall-less shacks near town he sees children his age or younger dressed like old people in caps and shawls, shucking oysters, their hands webbed with scars from the short, blunt knives they use. His father bartering the price of a half-bushel they will shuck together that evening. He learns the softness of his hands as he pries apart the algae-furred hinge. The taste of oysters like the whole sea on his tongue. The roar of his first hurricane when he is eight. His mother saying, *It will sound like a great big train.* Boats in the treetops the next day, their house flooded to the fourth step of the stairs. The girl on Deer Island who runs after her brother, screaming louder than the birds flocking overhead. Her family's pattern of return like that of the birds whose nesting grounds Isaac haunts, lying still for hours to watch the chicks emerge or the purple necks of the grown stretch and throb. There were some summers the family didn't come to Deer Island at all, but the birds always did. And if you told him he would live to see a day when the birds would not, their nesting grounds churned up and their eggs poisoned into jelly, he would've wished to die there and then.

Six

The day before he was to leave on the fifteen-hundred-mile journey to the School of Design in Providence, Rhode Island, Isaac took the cat-rigged skiff out of the bay and rode a good wind through the Dog Key pass, rounding by midmorning the western tip of Horn Island. He'd wanted to see a full day on the water, sunrise to sunset, before he gave himself over to the city and to studenthood, but he'd made himself wait that morning until his mother and father were up. It cost him sunrise, but he wouldn't leave them in the dark.

The common knowledge of his adoption didn't stop certain well-meaning fools in town from saying that Isaac resembled his father. And in the gathering light of the kitchen that morning, watching his father smile and stare out the window and light his first cigar of the day, Isaac might have believed it himself. At nineteen he'd grown taller than Ben, now married and a father-to-be, and, though no one said it, taller too than David had been. (Days before, when his mother had decided that David's room should be repainted for Ben's coming child, Isaac, who had only ever peered into the room, found himself dabbing paint over the notches that had marked David's height. And, seeing that the last was just at his forehead, he had to fight down a pull of guilt and, he hated to admit it, triumph.) His hours of rowing and swimming in the waters of the bay had made his shoulders thick and his chest deep. And, like the man who sat across from him at the table that morning, his time outdoors had tanned him, given him early lines about the eyes and mouth, a faint gold to the oak-brown hair.

He kissed his father on his unshaven cheek, told him when he would be back, and passing the stairs met his mother as she was coming down. Wrapped in nightclothes, the very same soft cloth she'd used to make blankets for the children she'd borne, she gathered this child not of herself, not even anymore a child, to her, before he was gone.

This was September, near the end of the trout spawn. He banked at inlets and coves on Horn Island, lay beside pools, and waded to his waist, sketching turtles and shorebirds with the pencil he otherwise wore around his neck on a string. In the afternoon he put his pad away and hung his pencil back, then he pushed out again.

He came through a misting rain of twenty minutes: windless, no need to put the sail down. When the rain was gone everything was dewy as dawn. He studied the play of light in the droplets that clung about the boat as he cut under the island, where he lowered his sail and rowed out to a grassflat off an unnamed point where the current broke both ways. He anchored there at the edge of the jade-green patch, where the deeper water muddled blue. Schools of mullet and white trout shot through the flat, shadows rippled over the clear patches of sand, and in their wake he knew would be speckled trout and other drum and, after them, catfish—hardheads and gafftops, barbed and onerous. At his feet was a covered pail of croaker minnows and shrimp he'd netted that morning and his fishing rod wrapped in oilcloth. Taking aim for the point so that he could reel through the grassflat, he baited a jighead with a minnow and cast. The line whipped to the pitch of the small inshore waves before the jighead hit and the line went taut with the motion of his reeling and the life that fought against it.

His family and several patrons of the arts in New Orleans who thought he had uncommon talent had pooled money and influence to put him in the notice of the academy, and his acceptance to the School of Design had been celebrated with an uncomfortably large party at the house of an old woman in the Garden District who had bought two of his paintings. There were songs and toasts, there were daughters to dance with in his fresh-pressed suit, his proud parents basking in it all. They seemed so ready for him to advance, to transcend them. He knew that he couldn't refuse to go, that to do so would spit in the face of everything they had given him. And though there were parts of him that wanted to learn, to be in a place where art was everywhere, wanted to be noticed and seen and, most of all, praised, going was a hard thing to face.

He painted for the same reason that he fished. The rod or the brush were bridges to the living world. He was only just beginning to understand this, what would be the direction of his art. To become closer with life, not to reproduce it from the eye of skeptic humanity. And to leave his home, the bay, the Gulf, he feared would mean the abandonment of everything he wanted to achieve in his work and as yet only dimly understood.

He fished into the afternoon and on the rising tide, pulling the anchor and rowing west of the point, then shipping the oars and casting over the grassflat as he drifted back.

To the west, off Cat Island, went a trio of boats no bigger than his own but without sails, rowed by fishermen who used handlines and kept the guesthouses and hotels supplied. He watched them bob against the reddening sky of afternoon, their arms reaching out and the lines that ran from them like veins into the water. Then he went back to his own casting and looking, losing himself for a while in chance and muscle memory.

When he looked up again, he found the fishermen were gone and a swift wall of dark-bellied clouds had rounded the bend in the shore, hugging tight to the coast. Black at their heart and roiled with electric purple, the clouds came on. He rowed out ahead of the island, into the pass, and raised the sail again. The wind was coming stronger now, as was the tide, and he could ride it in even without the sail, but the clouds had spread in a widening black hook, casting the water beneath them in darkness.

The first beads of rain fell on Isaac's face as he cleared the island, looking toward home, and he saw that the storm was on both sides of him. Two black horns driven by the crosswind. The waves began to cap and he felt his legs tense as he gripped the tiller. He could cut under the island and try to bank, ride out the storm there, or be driven inland through the Dog Keys by the current and hope not to be crushed on an oysterbed; he could fight into the wind above the island and anchor in deeper water while the storm, hopefully, spent itself inshore. Or he could race it back, cut straight through the horns. This was what he chose.

Half-standing, the wind at his back, he was in the gap of the pass between one island and the next when the storm overtook him. He held the mainline and whipped the boom to bank, but the tiller snapped like the neck of something living and the rudder jagged and flapped. He clawed to keep the boom, the boat spinning as he saw the last patch of clear sky, the one that he'd been heading for, swallowed by the storm. A vault of black that pulsed with strands of lightning, and beneath it the waters turned pale with some captured light from the sky above.

Out of the storm rose two pillars of water (he figured about a mile apart) shot through with a darkness deeper than that of the storm. Isaac held to what he could and, whirling, witnessed the waterspouts' advance. Sky and sea conjoined. He didn't hear the sail tear away but watched as it blew, full, across the water and was sucked up. The waterspouts were three now and thick as the smokestacks of the steamers he would see on calm days plying the horizon. But awesomely close to where he spun, now, unable to catch his breath.

In the moment before the boat capsized his head was thrown back and he saw the tower of water and the shapes of fish and the wreckage that perned at the heart of it. He looked up, his head screaming with wind.

According to what scale do we measure loss? Whether Isaac was alive or not, the rain would end and the waterspouts fade into mist. Fish sucked up into the atmosphere would be deposited miles inland, stunning farmers one week later, and the tide would wash the dead into rills and mounds on beachheads; summer would end and the patterns of the birds heading south would go on, the islands clustered with nests built by wintering dowitchers and terns, and the chill would hold the coast until it was knocked loose by the storms of February and March, then spring and spawn in the waters, the beached bodies of greenback and loggerhead turtles whose eggs are pearls of life waiting for the moon to call them out as it does the tides and our own blood, and the sea would warm and churn itself in summer storms again. Without him the life of the coast would go on unbroken and thoughtless as the breath now in your throat. But maybe the measure lies elsewhere, in a scale of another kind: In the moment, the next morning, when the battered catboat would be hauled to the Patterson's dock, its mast snapped and its belly pasted with sketches faded by the rain. Mrs. Patterson struck mute, her nails deep in her husband's arm while he fought beside the boat with the yachtsman who'd found it, clawing at the cleat and throwing off the rope as though he could cast the boat off and bring the boy back again.

Pushed landward by the current and the wind, Isaac swam. Could only catch so much of the rain-stung air. Farther in, he knew, lay oysterbars in razored humps hidden by the waves. He swam, trying to see ahead, trying to breathe, the boat long gone. His arms were getting weak and a numbness climbed his legs. Somewhere between the touch of ice and nothing at all. He wondered what it would feel like, the slowing of his heart, what thoughts cross when we know there won't be any more to follow. Then he saw it: the channel marker, bolt-upright in the waves. Something he could cling to, if he could. So he swam, kicking at the numbness that seemed to reach out of the water itself, and there was the rush of pain and relief when he smashed into the marker, scrambling to hold.

It was a postlamp mark, supported on four pilings, and it saved him. Arms and legs hooped, he climbed until he was above the waves and pulled himself into the crossbeams. There in the arms of the marker— for it was a living thing, covered in grass and algae and, lower, the barnacles that had raked him bloody—he stretched out, trying to balance his weight. Breathed.

The wind faded to a blow and as evening came he listened to the clank of the postlamp swinging overhead in its cage. When the moon rose he could look down and see the water like it was the bottom of a well. He nodded into sleep for a moment or an hour, bucked back awake to the sounds of whistle buoys and the moan of tugs. He shouted a few times for help, before his throat closed up.

Morning, oars slapped the pilings of the marker, and there were voices calling out to him in Spanish from a boat lashed below.

The men who found him were Isleños, recent immigrants from the Canary Islands, and had taken over the maintenance of the buoys and markers when the lighthouse-keeper had gone too arthritic to tend them. They had come to fill the postlamp after the storm and spotted the pair of bare legs dangling free. When he saw them, Isaac painfully unlatched himself from his perch and dropped down into the well of the water like a shot. He was laughing, in a dry-heave way, when they got him on board. *Insolada*, one said, and they laid him out with their lines and nets and the ten-gallon drum of kerosene for the lamp. He was naked save for his shredded trousers and the pencil still around his neck, scoured from throat to toe. They had no water aboard and so, while one man raised the anchor, the captain went among them and each man spat into his cupped hands in turn. Then the captain himself spat and went to where the boy lay, crouched over him and pressed his hands to the boy's cracked lips.

When he could speak he told them where he lived, but his voice and mind were weak and the Isleños had little English besides, taking him instead to the house on Deer Island. Too week to object when they, hollering, approached the small dock that extended off the Gulf side of the little island. Before the Isleños had tied off, the woman they privately called *La Reina*, but to her face (when they sold her fresh fish or octopus and who brought them cans of sweetmilk cut with strong coffee) was always Doña Marina, appeared from out of the great house and, when she saw the boy lying in the boat, fell immediately to giving orders.

They carried him unconscious up the dock and through the wide doors of the veranda and the sitting room, into a bedroom they assumed to be hers, where she waved for them to lay him out on the grand four-post bed. The women she'd engaged to clean and do her laundry once a week were not there, so it befell the men to do as she said, rummaging through her camphored cabinets in the dining room for linens and then wetting them in the basin so that she could wring the wet cloths over his mouth. The Isleños had heard a little of the gossip in town about this woman, who was said to have survived a shipwreck as a girl, and they believed none of it until now.

She, Marina, had survived much more than that. And she was keenly aware that her life up to this point, though insulated for many years by wealth, had been nothing if not an act of survival. Now here was this boy on her bed like a vision of an earlier time. When she was young, younger than him, she had been lost in these same waters, or not far off. Even bloody and sunburnt you could see he was well-formed, if not handsome. His hair was sun-bleached near his scalp but held to oaky brown in strands that fell across a faintly ridged forehead, shadowing eyes that might have been hazel. Not a round, boy-soft face, but not gawky or angled either. His body, or what she saw of it, had that unstamped quality of young men. He was perfectly ordinary. But then, she thought, why did it hurt to look at him?

She'd come here to escape for a little while the slow, grinding collapse of her family. The conflicts of her grown children, her sons, whose mutual resentment was lately honing into hate, and the conflicts of her own heart. So she would tell no one about the boy being brought there, not her husband, not even her daughter, Kemper, who was at school in New Orleans and would join them that year in Cuba for Christmas. This was a private sign that woke a private hurt, and it ached in her chest, all the echoed promise and pain of a life ahead.

When Isaac woke, the first face he saw was not Marina's, nor those of the men who'd saved him, but a framed portrait on the far wall to the left of the bedroom door. The subject was a girl, perhaps twelve, auburn-haired and seated in a flowered chair, wearing a high-necked blouse and an expression of supreme boredom. He rolled onto his side, body rocking with the remembered motion of the sea, and the girl in the portrait floated there with him.

He'd never been inside the house on Deer Island but the story of his family's ill-fated visit was repeated so often that he felt somehow he had. For the past two summers the woman, the mother of the girl in the portrait, had come alone. He would wave at her sometimes when he passed by in the boat and she would look up from her book and wave back. He lay there, listening to her talking in the next room, and then the woman's voice was gone and there were the voices of his parents and he thrashed to cover himself as they burst into the room.

Isaac tried to speak but his throat was a tight fist again, to be unclenched by aloe water in the coming days, and they swarmed him. His mother kissing him, forcing him back down with a strength he hadn't known she possessed; his father, moustache wet, nose running, held both his hands and shook them. Words of love and relief. Behind them hung the portrait of the bored girl, and through the half-open doorway he could see the woman, Marina, hazed with sunlight and indeterminate as the future.

PART 3

Daughter of the Sun

1914

One

It is coming in the warming water and the columns of the upper air. In the convergence of fronts and the tilting face of the sun. It is coming from the islands of the Cabo Verde west of Africa where the tradewinds, which once filled the sails of ships jammed with the captive and enslaved, make warlike commerce with other winds and form the beginnings of the storm. The hurricane, the god of the coast whose Passover is August and September, and which, before it was a god, was and remains a function of the earth's need to temper summer, a colossal cooling mechanism. Around these giants the weight of the world shifts, the atmosphere thins to vacuum, and were you to stand at the right height in one's eye you would be sucked skyward with the planet's hot updraft and dissolved among the mountainous clouds to fall as particles of rain. It is coming for them in the summer that begins with arrows and ends with the beginning of the Great War. And it has no name, the storm that will mark their coming together, for we did not always give names to storms and chart our expectations of them. Storms, like corporations, are only human in the intimacy of their destruction and the lives they mar. We can no more name the storm than we can hold the wind in our hands or know the nature of love. Try and you will find your fingers clawing emptiness, the weight of the world gone, and nothing between you and the void.

Isaac knew from the moment he saw her, screened by a cut of smooth cordgrass waving in the wind off the bay, that she was the one from the portrait. The shoddy painting on the wall of the bedroom in the Woolsack house on Deer Island—the daughter, Kemper. It had been years since that day, but he remembered. They were not ten yards from one another, in opposite cuts of the marsh, where he'd spent the better part of the afternoon sketching ribbed mussels and a needlefish sought by a crane, and she, it seemed, was poaching a crab trap.

When he rounded the bend she was shaking the trap in her hands, the wire clung with a few crabs, the others clattering in the bottom of her boat. She wore a cut-down cotton dress, her broad shoulders bare and sunburnt, and when she raised the trap and shook it he saw tufts of wet dark hair at the pale of her underarms. He'd shipped his oars and poled over with the broomstick he kept for that purpose. Jabbed the tip of the pole to halt his drift and stood watching her and the motion running through her.

When she saw him Kemper flung the trap overboard and it sank gurgling, rope and painted buoy snaking after. She looked up, glared through a sheen of sweat. An arc of hair fallen across her eye.

He recalled a story of some demigod who cried tears of reddened-gold.

She wiped the bottom-mud from her hands, smoothing down her hips, and gave him a look that swallowed him whole.

—Is that your trap? he said finally.

—Of course not. She sat down, never taking her eyes from him. At her feet the crabs were tearing at each other's arms. Is it yours? she said.

—No, but . . .

She let out a yelp and lifted her pinched feet up, the dress parting from the dimpled underside of her thigh. Cursing she grabbed the crabs by their pale blue swimfins and tossed them into a tin pail. He was laughing now and she gave him one last glance and grabbed her oars and pushed off, rowing deeper into the marsh.

He stood watching long after she'd gone, and he was drowning for the third time in his life.

He'd been back in Mississippi since June, having spent the first half of his twenties vagabonding after his expulsion from the School of Design. The wandering period came to an end one rainy morning in Mérida, in the state of Yucatán. That had been April of this year, when the Marines and Bluejackets were killing Mexican schoolboys in Veracruz, and he could no longer make excuses for his country, returning with as much distrust as when he'd left it. Starting out of Boston in late 1912, he'd traveled down into the peninsula of Florida, past the memory of the Boys' Home, to Tampa and from there to Havana and then Mexico. Tampico, Veracruz, and the peninsula where he sought out Mayan glyphs among the scrub creosote and waxthorn. He sent home brief letters, postcards forested with spiked plants and creatures unfamiliar to his parents. *At this rate*, Mr. Patterson remarked, holding up an envelope postmarked from a city in Mexico, *he'll be sketching penguins in Antarctica by Christmas*. But he'd come home after all, reclaimed the converted barn behind the house, where he threw himself into work, searching for his form, making palette-knife sketches while overhead the barncat Wildman lay dreamily on a beam, having resumed an old addiction to paint fumes. Isaac earned a little money working at the concrete and stonework business his brother Ben had started in Biloxi, designing and molding urns and birdbaths and fountains and laying walkways for the new crop of grand houses that had begun appearing along the seaside, mansions gnawing the sand and the grass with white-columned teeth. His mornings were of liquid stone and his afternoons given to paint and the coast, to the islands which welcomed him back with clouds of stinging insects, and he was happy until he was alone in bed at night. Then loneliness came creeping and the guilt of all he'd wasted and given up by leaving, how little he'd made of what he had been given. He was twenty-four or so.

At the School of Design he'd been saved from expulsion so many times, by well-meaning professors who claimed that his work—while decorative and lacking insight into what they insisted on calling the "souls" of his subjects—was worth pursuing, that when the last time finally came and they stopped saving him, Isaac was almost relieved. (There are plenty of artists, said the professor who broke the news to him, who can't find their way in the academy or the East Coast, plenty who have gone on to greatness outside these bounds. Though of course the man neglected to give an example of a single one.) His last day as a student was spent in the marble halls of a Bostonian industrialist's museum, milling at the back of a herd of classmates (those who would graduate with letters ingratiating them to New York, Paris, Rome) as his professor gave a haphazard walking lecture, lighting on one painting after another. Isaac stood for a long time before the second, smaller version of Copley's *Watson and the Shark*, on loan from such and such estate. The professor spoke of upright composition and romanticism and the heroic figurations of the white man in the waves and his would-be rescuers, and when the class moved on Isaac remained, transfixed not by the men but by the shark. A bloated misconception with all the life of a half-rotted specimen in a jar. Isaac had seen a reproduction plate of this painting before, in some book, and as far as he knew Copley had never seen a live shark—maybe a blacktip hauled stinking onto a Back Bay dock. The shark in the painting was no shark at all but the sum of the fear and revulsion of a man who'd never seen one. Nature as horror, the numinous made obscene. And standing there amid the drifting shoals of other patrons, more than in all the snowy hours he'd spent in Providence, he wanted desperately to be south, on the water; he longed to see a shark again. He left not long after, and by early 1913 was in New York among the crowds at the American Exhibition, the fabled Armory Show, where he saw, among other visions which left him sick with possibility, the hares of de Souza Cardoso, a young Portuguese who would die a few years later in the influenza pandemic. The form that is not approximation but essence, the line capturing motion and the pattern of being, which he'd see again in the carved Mayan of gods who were neither man nor animal but both.

In Port Tampa, Cuban fishermen had let him help in the skinning of a shark. He learned how to prepare the meat, the three long soaks that made the flesh edible (the same, he would find in Mexico, was true of the stingray, whose meat is as delicate as a scallop's when treated right), the stewing in tomato and chili pepper, Creole red and spiced with clove like the food he'd grown up on. He ate with the fishermen and watched as the sun set in the direction he was headed for, glad, for all the familiarity of taste, to have his thoughts drowned in a language not his own.

When he saw her the next morning Kemper Woolsack was on the beach shooting arrows into the back of a parlor chair. The bowstring notes reaching him on the water so that he broke from his course and rowed to the eastern tip of Deer Island. She stood in bloomer pants cinched at the knees, calves caked with sand, her shirt untucked and billowing. She'd tacked a paper target to the winged back of the chair, a bullseye drawn with lipstick, and she was firing into the red.

Kemper pinching blossoms of fletch from an umbrella stand sunk in the sand at her feet, seemingly indifferent to this person walking his boat through the surf, though the memory of his stained linen shirt, open at the neck, and the vague urge to smell it, hadn't left her since the day before.

Isaac heard the twang of the string and the thwack of the arrow striking home and the keel of his boat hissing gently in the sand as he pulled it onshore.

She angled her hips to better guide the shots, the freckled muscle of her shoulder bunching as she drew back, then the arrow was gone and the echo of release shuddered through her body. The arrowhead buried in spring and cushion, ruining a fine, expensive chair because why not. She looked like the wild survivor of some near-apocalypse, careless of the value that things once had, as if somewhere not far she had a smoldering pile of banknotes for a campfire.

—Well, she said.

—Do you want to come out on the water?

—Now?

—Sure.

—I don't even know you.

—You used to throw shells at me, he said. Chase me off the beach. Right over there.

She looked in the direction he was pointing as if to catch a glimpse of her childhood self between the dunes.

—Did I ever get you? she said.

—Oh sure, he said. All the time.

Slow waves rolled into the marsh, Isaac before her rising and falling with them. He like a doorway suddenly thrown open to her, saying, Come on. It was bad enough for Kemper to recall her past, because that meant thinking of her family, who hadn't been in the same room together for years. That spring she'd graduated from Newcomb College, a New Orleans women's school much enamored with social engineering along the lines of Vassar and Agnes Scott, and now she was in the first leg of what she hoped would be a yearlong ramble culminating in some, she hoped further, substantial personal change. She had no commitments, no fiancé, no burning passion to do good or ill in the world. She just wanted to *see*. And before she went a way she didn't know, she wanted to gather herself in a place she did, in the summer house, and if not know herself then know what she was leaving. But here was Isaac, who she didn't really know at all, saying he remembered her.

The water was calm and she sat at the stern crowded with tackle while Isaac rowed them to the grassflats between Dog and Cat Islands. He sat at the bow, outstretched legs tensing as he rowed. His bare feet, long and thin, the hair on his toes pale gold.

At first she kept her own legs drawn to her chest, but bit by bit she allowed herself to ease, her feet coming nearer to his with every jut of the boat, until she was brushing his ankle with the high pitch of her arch. They spoke as if this was not happening—their first secret—making small talk while she pressed him like a pedal and he thought he might go mad.

Then they were floating above an underwater meadow, the water around them an eye of milky green in the darker face of the bay. Beds of turtle grass whose roots formed an undergrowth where crabs and pale larval shrimp and wavering starfish fed on particles of grass broken down by still-smaller organisms, and higher, in the lilting canopy, fish darted and fed on the life below.

They took turns casting and rowing out to drift back over the flats, and when she boated a good-sized Spanish mackerel Isaac dropped the anchor and scooted over to help her unhook the fish, an arrow of silver skin dotted along the midline with green the color of summer grass, but before he could draw out the hook she did it herself and snapped the mackerel's neck on the gunnel. Smiling, she handed the fish over and he brought it back with him to the bow, where he took from his knapsack a knife and, she realized after a puzzled moment, a lime.

She watched him gut the fish and pitch its bright entrails overboard, how he cut below the gills tracing back along the jagged points of its spine, followed by a deeper cut along the contour of the ribs, raising the fillet. He flipped the fillet and in one smooth stroke freed the flesh from the skin, which he laid out before him like a plate and set the fillet on it, cutting the meat into pieces.

—Raw? she said.

He held up the knife as though to say hold on, and he quartered the lime and squeezed its juice through his fingers over the pieces of fish.

The smell of blood and seawater and citrus. The sun warm on her back, light washing over her and onto the surface of the water where now and then little breaths of bubbles broke.

He held a piece out to her and she took it. Up close the meat was pearly, white striations in the waves of muscle. A moment before, it had been whole and moving. She ate the first and it was all ocean-clean and sun-bright bursts of lime. He ate his piece and asked if she liked it, and there was a moment when she might've cried, might've said she'd never tasted anything better in her life, that it was everything. But she only nodded and took another piece for herself, watching him watch her eat. There would be time enough to tell him later, and she would tell him everything.

That evening he slept beside her on the veranda of the Deer Island house, curled on the chaise whose cushions were streaked with salt and smelled strongly of mold. A bitter tang above the warmth of his breath. She woke first, at twilight, afraid to move, his hand wedged under her back, and unmoving she watched the last of the gulls circling between the island

and the main and studied the shape of his body, his shoulders, the rise of his ass. When he woke she was asleep again, and his awe and exhaustion kept him still. She lay with one arm bent behind her head, cheek resting on a wrist as thick as his, and he could see by the twitch of her mouth, her fluttering lids, that she was dreaming. There was nothing pliant in her, nothing weak. He loved already how he couldn't encompass her waist, the strength that flared in her back when she rolled atop him. She would not be steered.

He wondered at the nature of her dream, which did not, by the look on her face, seem pleasant, and he lay beside her as you might a dying fire in the morning cold, though the air was boiling even in the dark.

Two

The last time her family had been together, the last time they ever would be, was in Havana during Christmas 1910. The place whose conqueror claimed was once home to a people with wings and feathers. A lie, of course, like the images of gold-laden rivers and willing native maidens and a people without morals or history. But the name survived: Avian. Avan. Havana. Kemper had read this once in a book about Columbus, and the idea, like Havana itself, never ceased to fill her with sadness. Whenever she thought of it, whenever she was in Havana—so like New Orleans and yet something Kemper could never possesses, never be a part of—the claim made her and all who'd come after seem unremarkable and wonderless. A people who walked where others once had flown.

From her bedroom in her family's house in the Vedado, Kemper could look out over the lengths of flower garlands and Japanese lanterns strung across the courtyard and hear the waves beat the breakers and glimpse through the gaps of nearby roofs the faint forms of sea-birds riding the wind. Gulls glancing off the quayside and dipping into the bay still blighted by the old and unremoved wreck of the U.S.S. *Maine*. The destruction of her family as she knew it would commence the following day, the last fragile bonds they, the children, had maintained into adulthood irrevocably broken, but for now they were coming together.

Her brother, Angel, had come from Nicaragua. He was the one she was closest to, and that day he'd sat with her for a while and talked about the things that had gone wrong, and some that had gone right, in his life. Now he was resting in his own room, maybe writing a letter. Her mother and father were together somewhere, talking, drinking, having broken the fast of separation they maintained most of the year. (Of course, none but the most docile and domestic of her friends' parents spent more than a few months together. A consequence of wealth.) Red was in the city apparently with friends from Louisiana State University, who'd come to watch their football team play the University of Havana on Christmas morning. Red had yet to see his older brother, and Kemper wasn't looking forward to the little tensions and contests that came whenever the brothers shared space. Red's jockeying for the foremost place in their father's line of sight. The threat of outburst that had hung over him from the time he was a boy.

Whatever the case, tonight they'd all go to mass and she would sit between her brothers, feeling awkward and rangy, made painfully aware that she was as big or bigger than both of them, breathing the air of their mutual distrust; the three of them forming with their parents a line of fair severity, a red-gold gash in the rows of dark-haired people gathered there to celebrate a strange and unattainable family. Then they'd come home and have a late dinner, and in the morning go to the baseball at the Almendares Park, sit in the president's box, her father murmuring darkly with some dignitaries, and watch Louisiana boys stomp Cuban boys while in the stands American sailors and travelers cheered.

Looking out, she thought of the *Maine*, whose carcass she'd seen that day when her steamer from New Orleans anchored in the harbor of Havana. The explosion of the *Maine* had given the United States reason at last to intervene in the Cuban revolt, and so her country had taken, won, and changed the name of the war. The Spanish-American War. Her mother, Cuban-born and exiled since the American Civil War, took no joy in this intervention, no sorrow in the loss of the ship, even when the ribbons were being tied and the flags unfurled, the nation reeling less at the scale of death than the quaking shock to national pride—the knowledge that now we could be wounded in an instant, and in an instant via humming wires know the extent of our vulnerability. She remembered hearing her mother say the U.S. had dressed Cuba as a woman in torn clothes on the verge of being raped, then kindly shoved Spain out of the way and taken our turn. Kemper guessed she must've been around seven or eight when she heard that.

In her family's house, she thought of the bodies that had been trapped in the belly of the *Maine*. Floating eyeless in the dark (such was the concern of the nation for this emblem and the martyred dead that it would be another two years before the ship and its death-load would be hauled out into the Gulf and sunk), their tomb rusting, snarled with the garbage of the city, mainmast jutting askew and to whose crow's nest dared boys would swim and climb, pumping their fists, until they were fired on by the soldiers and sailors from Camp Columbia, Americans who'd been called back to quell the black rebellion of 1905 and the white liberal revolt of the next year and never left.

Below, the servants were lighting the lanterns, little blooms of fire in orange paper globes. Fragile houses, she thought, for something as strong as fire. She heard her parents' voices from downstairs, then her brothers'. The gulls were gone, too dark to see, and she stepped back from the window, feeling suddenly dizzy, the walls of the house seeming very much like paper themselves. And she a ball of flame.

—Where are you? Isaac says.

—Right here. With you.

Which is not entirely true. She is shaking off the past, her memories, as you might shake off sleep.

They are standing together in the kitchen of the house on Deer Island, a lamp burning between them against the early morning dark. Her gaze has drifted off, waiting for the kettle to boil. When it shrieks she lifts the kettle from the red disc, pours a fall of steaming water between them soaking coffee grounds, clove, peels of cinnamon. While the coffee steeps she unwraps a loaf of sugar and with a kitchen knife chips off white arrowheads that glitter dully in the lamplight. She picks the last of the blood oranges from the crate and tells him to take the bell from the lamp. When he's done this Kemper passes the orange through the naked flame, rolling the bruised-looking skin around the fire, humming.

—What are you doing?

—Waking the peel, she says.

The orange smoking in her hand, first she rubs its skin with one arrowhead of sugar, then the other, moving to a private music as her fingers travel from the indent of the stem to the pursed tip. Setting the burnt orange aside, she drops the arrowheads into their cups and fills them with the spiced coffee.

He leans into her, head swimming. He has drifted into his own past, all of which seems to lead up to this, to her.

—It's perfect, he says.

Once she would've written Angel, her brother, and told him everything. She'd done this, written him her secrets, from the time she was a girl (when she had no real secrets at all) and had kept on writing him for a time even after the night in Havana when he left them all forever.

His secrets, his life, were another matter. They required complete circumspection in person and in print. By his mid-thirties Angel Woolsack had mastered lies and truth and the pregnant gap between them. He lied for the family business, the lines of ships and rail and the gold fruit that grew along the railways hanging in hands from trees which are not trees at all, he'd told her once, but the tallest grasses in the world. And Angel did worse things than that, she knew, for Americans' fruit was bought with quite a lot of other peoples' blood. But more than anything, he lied in order to survive. It was his air and language, the avoidance of truth, so he seemed always on the verge of a revelation, which gave him a kind of gravity that drew her unerringly to him, the little sister who envied what she imagined to be the freedom of his life in Nicaragua, before she understood—if not accepted—what he was. He never told her outright, but there came a time when she realized what lay behind how he politely deflected her questions about marriage, women. For a time in her teenage years she'd thought him sexless, the force of her own desires so urgent and evident, like rashes on the surface of her skin, that his silence, the absent pronouns, seemed bizarre. But by that Christmas, their last together, after Midnight Mass, while the rest of the family rode and she walked with Angel back to the house in the Vedado, she knew enough and he trusted her enough that she could ask about his friend in León.

—Doing very well, Angel said. We saw each other last week.

She took his arm and said that was good. You might say she managed to say it, because no matter how hard she tried, the thought of one man loving another disturbed some small fixed part of her. Sent her into little spirals of denial. But if she couldn't bring herself to say this, any more than he could bring himself to say his lover's name, she could and did say that she hoped they were happy.

Angel squeezed her arm and then changed the subject to a poem he said reminded him of her. Promised he would read it to her, to them all, that night at dinner. But he did say, as they walked, that what she had said was kind, really kind.

There was no kind word then, nor are there many now, for what Angel Woolsack was. Which state of being still carried the death penalty in much of the world that considered itself civilized, the world for whom he broke governments and manned machine guns from Nicaragua to the borders of British Honduras. Among the men he knew, friends and lovers, men of property who met under the auspices of literary clubs and salons and leftist groups, the term "modern" was common. They had wives, many of them, these elites who'd gone to military schools and read more Verlaine than von Clausewitz, and some enjoyed women as much as they did men, or they constructed elaborate systems and excuses, but he didn't feel much like this kind of modern man. More that he was displaced, stateless, out of time, which was still preferable to how he'd felt as a boy: cursed, malformed, but never, as another popular euphemism went, confused. Of course he'd tried to rid himself of wanting who and what he wanted, took himself apart as he would a Maxim or a Hotchkiss gun, but when the pieces were reassembled he was the same. He loved who he loved and was hopelessly, helplessly bound to it.

And at this time he had a shifting cast of lovers, was open to fate-fraught encounters that happened sometimes at hotel baths or on long journeys by ship or train, the met glance that says I want what you want, the electric thrill of being chosen (though these often ended poorly, which meant at worst violence, or at best sadness hard on the trail of pleasure). But all that was changing. In the past year he'd met the man he would always return to: Eduard Chamorro de Aviles, son of a prominent Nicaraguan family, landowners whose holdings you could walk from the Pacific coast and across the volcanic ranges to the shores of the Caribbean with little interruption. Eduard kept his wife and children in Managua, where his uncles held positions in government. He and Angel had met at a flat in León, saw each other from opposite sides of a room filled with would-be poets and other such fortunate sons. He was literate and warm, Eduard, his features round and smooth as his voice; small about the hips and shoulders, he had a dark tuft of hair at his chest that tightened into curls when he sweat. He could laugh, easily, freely, and this was what Angel loved more than anything.

He squeezed his sister's arm, for he'd come to the point he never could quite cross. The point of saying outright what he knew she must already know. So they walked together into the old neighborhood, passing other people, couples, families, carrying within themselves the dread and happiness of grown children going to see the people who'd made them.

Angel's life was one of consummate control broken up by intervals of discrete and shuttered joy. But even in his rawest moments, with Eduard, whom he loved, when they were in some shabby room rented by the hour in the worst parts of León and he could let his guard slip and was, for an hour or a night, the man he knew himself to be, there was yet at his core a dark, tight knot of untruths that had been there for so long he'd begun to believe some of them himself.

The worst of these lies stemmed from a scar he had on his left arm, just below the shoulder. A scythe-shaped mark that hadn't been stitched and so showed a wide pink grin. The scar was visible only if he was shirtless and you were close to him, say between his arms. And such scars, little portals to our pasts, invite questions from those we've let close.

Eduard, mouth love-slack, asking —Where did you get that scar? Is it from a battle?

—From someone I loved, Angel said.

—Oh?

—He was angry. Jealous. We had an argument. He had a knife.

—Was he an American?

Angel said that he was, though we're all Americans, aren't we, love? And he told the story, the lie, that the boy had been a year behind him at school and they'd been lovers, a menacing secret kept between them, and when Angel was going to leave and broke off their affair, the boy in a jealous rage had grabbed a letter-opener from his table and slashed Angel across the arm, begging him to stay or take him along.

—And did you?

—I was bleeding, Edu.

And Eduard had sighed the way Angel had learned a man would when he told this version of the story. The sigh called up by the version of himself that was desired, wanted, wounded, strong. Eduard had pressed into him and fallen into a deep midday sleep but Angel lay awake with the lie like another presence in the bed. The truth was he'd been the one a year behind, in love with an older boy on the same dormitory floor; they'd written poetry together whose pronouns masked the truth of their feelings; spent nights up; jerked each other with unpracticed ferocity; and he had been the one who'd come apart when the older boy was poised to graduate and leave; he'd been the one in tears, begging to be taken along. And when the boy suddenly became another person, no longer the poet, no longer the love, and said to Angel that he was a pest, that he needed to get out, it had been Angel who took a glass from the sideboard and smashed it on the lip of the table and, pleading, raked the broken edge across his arm. *This is how much I love you. See?*

He might have never told the story at all, but he'd come to rely so much on the false version of himself that the truth and the pain were bound up in the lie that was his life.

Angel at the dinnertable, reading them the poem. He said it was political (their father gave a little groan) but not to worry about that. Just listen to the words. The poem was by the great Nicaraguan writer Rubén

Darío, and had been published in León a few years back. The lines he read spoke of Our America, a place of hurricanes and love, and was addressed to men with Saxon eyes and barbaric souls, to whom the poet insisted Our America (*Whose?* Red mumbled) lives . . .

—*Y sueña. Y ama, y vibra; y es le hija del Sol.*

Kemper saw her father looking to her mother.

—Daughter of the sun, her father said. Damn, that's not half bad.

—Read it again, Angel, her mother said.

And he did, his voice so comfortable in Spanish, the tiredness about his eyes easing for a moment.

—Whose America? Red said. He keeps saying *Ours.*

—He means Spanish America, doesn't he?

—Right, Angel said and tucked the clipping back into his coat pocket. But that's the thing, isn't it? What's ours and what's theirs isn't the question. It's who we are and what America is.

—Daughter of the sun, their father said, raising his glass.

Red sat back, arms folded. Kemper could see something working darkly in him.

—Well, I don't know about Saxon eyes or what, Red said. But it's *ours* one way or another.

At just past three on Christmas day Kemper rose from her seat in the president's box at Almendares Park and left in the last minutes of the game. Left Red, who was howling along with the other Americans in the crowd, left her mildly embarrassed parents, and left Angel, who she hoped would come with her, but didn't. As she made her way out of the stands she saw, coming to their level, the Louisiana players being borne out of the stadium and to parties that carried on through the night at taverns and barracks, hotels and the houses of diplomats and magnates, one of which Red would later attend and where he would get viciously drunk. She walked on, joining the streams of Cuban fans who went with clenched jaws past corners dotted with U.S. Marines, the people around her stricken with that dazed outrage that comes with losing. You wish for nothing more than to go and hide yourself away but your city is overrun with these people, veins throbbing in their square heads as they greet each other with the chant they'd kept up throughout the game: *Lick the spics! Kill the spics! Rah! Rah! Rah! Louisiana!*

Kemper hurrying back to the house, keeping her head down, hating everything as all around her went roaring Americans, recounting the plays and hits and the score—*Sixty-six to goddamn nothing!*—hearts bursting with the rightness of the outcome, reveling in the affirmation of everything they believed to be true about themselves.

When she reached the house in the Vedado, Kemper shut herself away in her room. And she would be there when her parents and Angel trickled back, and throughout the rest of the evening, listening as their three voices pared to two, her mother heading off to bed, the rising scent of tobacco smoke like childhood itself both rank and remarkable. She was almost asleep when the soldier came knocking at their door.

The soldier, she would learn later, was not a soldier at all but a Marine assigned to consular duties, dispatched on the unenviable task of telling a very rich man that his son had gotten into some violent trouble at the consulate's house and would his father, sir, please come and get him.

Now she was on the landing of the main stairway watching Angel and her father at the door. The Vs of sweat in their backs as they stood in the doorway, their shoulders dropping at something she couldn't quite make out. Then they were gone and the house was silent again. Kemper listened for her mother's stirring but heard nothing. Her mother had the habit of staying in bed regardless of the commotions of a night, which on the one hand was wonderful for children prone to sneaking out, but also made them question if she cared about them at all. Kemper went to her room and dressed, pinned up her hair, then back downstairs to the study, and she would be there an hour later when they returned, bearing Red between them.

Of all things, he was smiling. While their father cursed the door and Angel said Christ, Red, slurring, gleefully damned them both. When they hauled Red into the parlor where Kemper sat waiting, the faces of the two who held him went tense with embarrassment, and then Red caught sight of her too and what he did to his face put her heart in her throat.

Smiling had come hard for Red Woolsack, a mystery among the mysteries among the din of emotions of his childhood, the myriad expressions faces wore, the understanding of which was available to everyone, it seemed, but him. Poor Red, they said. Poor Georgie. Their faces bewildering signals. Another language. What others did without a second thought, Red acquired through effort. But even still there were times when his efforts couldn't overcome what he lacked. He'd spent hours before the mirror on his dresser, training his face to smile, sometimes with a picture at hand or with the memory of how his brother or sister had done it. Kemper had caught him once, practicing at his mirror, and he would never forget the look of disgust on her face, hovering there behind him in the glass. That look he understood perfectly.

Now Red had shaken loose of them and was stalking about the parlor, calling everyone bastards, everyone on this lousy, shitting island. Angel saying to keep his voice down for Christ's sake, holding his own to a low growl. His shoulders shaking. She'd seen her brothers fight more times than she could count, feeling in those encounters the vague sense that they were moving toward some dark height, something final, and whereas before they had never reached it, she saw that this time would be different.

Then they were on each other, grappling, their father trying to thrash and elbow his way between them. Upending reading lamps and furniture and the ashtray beside her, so that Kemper had to leap from the chair. A cloud of ash wafting now, though the only thing burning was them. A decanter cracked on the tile and her mother was behind her, screaming for them to stop, calling them boys. Her father's hands in their faces now, finally able to pry them apart, howling,

—Enough!

The brothers, separate but moving with an awful grace that told her the pause would not last. Kemper reached out an arm to catch her mother, watching the rise and fall of her father's chest, seeing his eyes flicker past her to the woman who had borne these children and the three dead who'd come between, the woman he'd known longer than anyone else alive and who loved them all with something greater than rage and greater than life. In what she would later think of as her first act as an adult, Kemper took her mother's hands in hers and held them as long as she could.

Her brothers like dancers, on their toes.

—You through now, George?

—Hell no, you sonofabitch.

—Shut your mouth. Angel cut his eyes to their mother and back to Red. Don't you care?

—You think plugging banana niggers makes you a man?

—You're a child.

Red, lifting his chin, as though to see out of the depth he'd reached, said,

—You're a faggot.

She saw Angel's jaw go slack as Red, bouncing now, raked the word over his voice again. Spat. And to the side of them, falling back, their father, whose face was suddenly that of the old man he would soon become: all outraged confusion at these creatures he had held and hoped for and that could find no sole object or direction, as though the known world reared up and tore away its own face, a mask. He stared into it, where it hid behind his children's eyes. His voice faint and lost.

—A what? he said.

The word dropped broken among them. It had not yet entered common usage and was known then only to portions of the young. Angel was partway across the floor when Red fixed on their father and told him what it meant.

As his brother spoke, Angel Woolsack in that moment lived the nightmare that had stalked the dark periphery of his life. Flooded with dread that might have been a kind of sick relief if the moment itself did not so completely resemble the nightmare. Everything he'd ever suspected, about what others thought, about what others would think of him, was there before him confirmed in all their faces as Red spoke. Spat. Saying, —He fucks *boys*, Dad. That's what.

Joseph Woolsack, collapsing into himself, stared at his youngest son. Then with a speed that marked the last of his youth, he covered the distance between himself and Red and struck his son so hard that his long copper hair waved limp as he fell, stunned, to the floor.

—You're disgusting, Joseph said once and then again. I won't have it. I won't have it said—

Red sitting up, glaring past his father, aiming for his brother's face. —Go on. Say you don't, faggot.

At this point Joseph looked to Angel. At this point, in a life spent searching every corner of every human being he encountered for the betrayal he knew to be inevitable, Joseph Woolsack looked to his oldest son. He would have believed nothing, would have torn this house and everything near him apart before he believed it, had he not seen the plain truth in Angel's face. The face that favored him most of all. And there in the child to whom he had revealed the most of himself, whose similarities he coveted, the betrayal was made manifest. And now he'd struck down the one who told, who sat up now saying, See—*See*. And he was father to them both, the betrayer and the one who told.

He stood there and could not bring himself to move, though he wanted more than anything something else to strike. Something other than his children. He thought of falling on himself, beating his own face into unrecognizable pulp. Erasing the self that had made them. He thought of the smoke that had risen from his own father's head, the back of the old man's skull blown away, as he'd watched from the doorway of his father's office when he was a boy of eleven.

Angel now so utterly swallowed in nightmare, wanting one word, one glance, to draw him out, to give him a reason not to do what every cornered outraged fiber of him screamed for. He tried to meet his sister's eyes, wanting her to say something, anything, for him. He looked to her, gave her this chance, and she, like the rest of them, failed him.

Kemper held her mother who'd begun to weep and it was all she could do to contain her as Angel went for Red, moving with a liquid, murderous calm. Her mother clawing at her neck until Kemper shoved her back and ran, drawn to her brothers, who had now reached the place they'd been heading for all their lives. She, hating them both, threw herself into this violence. Catching Angel before he got to Red, snatching his arm as he tried to bat her back. The brother who shared her secrets, who was her light in all this darkness. Kemper, choking his arm as hard as she could, screaming in his face to stop. All of them together now and screaming. But it was her voice and what she said as she fought him that she would remember. Crying out,

—Leave him alone. Leave him—God—*leave!*

◆ ◆ ◆

Angel Woolsack left his family that night, carrying with him nothing but what he wore, his billfold in his jacket pocket. Weeks later he arrived in Nicaragua, and in León he took a room in one of the familiar questionless places, paid the boy who came to change the pot to deliver a message he'd scrawled on the back of a postcard addressed to Eduard.

I'm here, he wrote. *Come find me.*

If you've ever been bodily hurt, you know what it means to have someone you love come and care for your wounds. The same applies to wounds of the soul. First your reluctance, the shame, and then the warm flood of care and the surrender of your strength. When you are hurt but otherwise whole, there is nothing more comforting than this. Nothing so intimate, that jolts you through with need and pushes the blood low. Another's hand dabbing and wiping, fingers spread at the base of your back. New wounds that will heal, some vanishing back into skin, and others scarring, joining with the old.

He sat naked before Eduard, watching him wring out the rag in the basin the boy had brought. Saw his eyes take in the sum of his wounds and linger for a moment on the scythe-shaped scar on his left arm.

—Wait, Angel said.

Eduard paused, the only sound the trickle of the rag in his hand.

—I want to tell you how I got this, he said, cupping his hand over the scar.

—You've told me, love.

Angel Woolsack, no longer himself, said he hadn't. Said he'd lied.

—Let me tell you really.

Three

For the next month Isaac made daily trips to Deer Island, most often by boat but there were many other times too, warm mornings, windless nights, bright afternoons, that saw him swim. If the sun was out he wore an old bathing suit, and whenever he pulled himself up onto her dock or walked up the beach to meet her, Kemper would run to him and press her mouth to his chest, sucking the moisture from the fabric of the suit. Other times he packed his clothes in an oilcloth sack and towed them as he swam. So he came to know the worth of his body as she shaped him, claimed him, with her words.

Your shoulders, she would say. Your back. Your legs. Your neck.

Her voice which was many voices, accents, tones—a country unto itself. And she said so much, encompassed him so totally, that all he could say back was, *Yours*.

At the School of Design he'd been required to study himself, make endless portraits, sketches, sculptures; hours spent staring at what interested him the least in all the world. But when she touched him, when she spoke, it was as though he hadn't known he had a body until now. She could sense his surprise and the need that went along with it, to be in her presence, to be a body. If not for the fact of her want, she thought, he might happily melt into the water or blow away like the grains of sand on the wind.

And though she wanted him, she needed just as much to be alone. Years later they would meet a diver who told them about how, after coming up from the deepest wrecks, he would have to spend time in an iron chamber before he could breathe real air. When she heard this she realized that was what it had been like: she had to spend time without him those early days or else her blood would have crackled in her veins.

Their hips were bruised, their lips were sore, so that even when they were apart there was the ache of connection. As a girl she'd gone through a phase of pain, when even the lightest touch, a snapping doorknob, a cabinet lip, would make her cry with pain, until one day her father roared that he would have the whole goddamn house padded if she didn't stop. He never did, and the pains went away as quickly as they'd come, but she felt more and more like the padding of her life had been stripped away and now everything was raw and real.

She woke one night after Isaac had gone, smelling his wet footprints on the tiles in the dark, and she was left with the realization that these were the last times she would wake alone.

She is on the boat with Isaac, reeling in a bluegill, when the shark comes to them. A shadow from deeper water. The shark, sensing the fish suddenly snatched out of its path, had changed course and followed as the bluegill fought against this unknown force, followed the disruption into the shallow waters of the grassflat and now as the fish seems to leap away into the lighted upper water and is gone, in frustration, circles the mystery of the boat.

She says for him to look, but he already is. Both of them are.

When the shark turns, the whole of its back comes above the water-line, skin patterned in stripes like shadows over sand, twice the length of the boat, which, when the crescent tail of the shark strikes the anchor-line, begins to rock.

Isaac crawls toward her, takes the bluegill still hooked to her line and pitches it into the basket with the rest of their catch, never taking his eyes from the shark. And she cannot look away either, even as he takes her hand, mistaking, in the moment, awe for fear. She watches in wonder at being so suddenly and irrevocably reduced—uncentered from the universe.

The shark hasn't broken its circuit and will not for some time. In the interim she finally turns and looks at Isaac and slides with him down until they are stretched on their sides in the belly of the boat, separated from each other by a breath and by an inch of lapstraked wood from the shark, still circling. They are no longer afraid: they are not hiding but coming closer—to each other and the water and the thing whose passage they feel but cannot see and to whose motion they soon add their own.

When she told him about her brother, the one who was gone, Isaac said the first thing that came to him, something he hoped would help but which fell dead and awkward as soon as it left his tongue.

—No, Kemper said. If he forgave me he would've said something. He would've written me back. But he just . . . left . . . Like I told him to.

—He might, though.

—It's been four years, Isaac. Four years. No one's heard from him.

—Still.

She was quiet for a while, then she asked if Isaac had ever known anybody who was *like that*.

—A few.

—How did you know?

He thought for a moment. —They didn't say anything. You just know.

She lay with her back to him, her face faint in the glass of the French doors glazed with the setting sun. Her birthday was not far away, a date normally meaningless, but this birthday, her twenty-first, marked the date when she would come into her shares in the company. In a few days she would go to New Orleans and the offices of Gulf Shipping & Fruit to sign the forms, and this knowledge pushed her further into silence.

—Come on, he said. Let's go out on the water.

Storms at the end of Kemper's fingers, trailing the surface of the water otherwise still for miles around. They were in the grassflats, Isaac had the anchor set, and he went to the bow and leaned with her, shadowing her hand as it stirred the water. Their water.

Your water too, however changed it may be. And from where they sat off the eastern tip of Cat Island the air was clear enough that you could see the water darkening in bands toward the horizon, the shadow of the falling slope of the continent, the end of the land which even then drained from its corn-choked heart streams of poison, nitrates flushed downward by the great floodplain, the river, and fed into the Gulf, and which in the days to come would grow to an obscene fertility, reaching its height some ninety years later when the runoff of a vast monoculture and that of a nation of bright green lawns mounded with the waste of well-fed pets all sluiced down concrete gutters to the hemmed and hobbled creeks which feed into the rivers which feed into the Gulf where, offshore, algae breeds, an explosion of hyperlife as diatoms gorge and multiply and die, their minute corpses drifting down through zones of light and shadow, sinking to the black reaches where there is no light but what comes from certain creatures and the beams of stray automatons seeking vents or oil seeps, the pale, husked bodies settling like snow in drifts on the seafloor, and mats of bacteria rimed with veins of sulfur broad as interstate lanes consume what is left of the dead and themselves multiply and die, starving the water of oxygen so that a layer of cooler, denser water runs beneath the flow of life, and any living thing that passes here joins the empire of death, surfacing in great rafts of corpses that sometimes block shipping lanes or wash onto the shores of the states bordering the Gulf, which themselves, like the dead, dense water that lies beneath the sea we imagine to be filled with life, are invisible to the consideration of the country above them: death fed by life fed by the belief that there must be regions into which we pour our poison as we drift thoughtless as lovers in a small boat, focused only on each other, our minds far from what we will not live to see or what is removed from us by distance and time.

Four

On Monday, 3 August 1914, Isaac rode first class with Kemper to New Orleans. The talk on the train was of a storm that had come into the Gulf and, more, of the greater storm sweeping over Europe, the declarations of war falling one after another, until there was only Britain left, and the United States, watching for now. The world as they knew it held a gun to its head. The following Wednesday Kemper would sign the papers for her shares in the family company, and she didn't want Isaac there for that, though she wouldn't tell him as much, and besides he'd promised his brother that he would come back to help with a large fountainpiece at the shop, so in the meantime, and with a modicum of intrigue, they got a room at the Grunewald, which they rarely left except in the evenings to eat at half-deserted restaurants, walk the streets, the sparse parks, the levee, and, once, on Tuesday the fourth, to visit the Museum of Art, where she insisted he take her to see the paintings of his entered in the next year's exhibition. After a while of Kemper badgering the docents and attendants and the curator himself, they were taken down a hallway overgrown with pipefittings to the storage room where the paintings awaiting display were kept. He cut the paintings free of their twine and brown paper bindings and stood back beyond the reach of the light while Kemper held them up one by one to the bulb. Her face was so close to the canvases that she might have been searching for flecks of dust in the brushstrokes, a story in the layering that made up the image itself.

She saw the brushstrokes were not even strokes of whole tone but infinite particles of color. Bursts and waves that fused together the farther she was away.

The larger canvas was of a storm, a waterspout stretched between sea and sky like black spittle in a giant's mouth; the smaller was a portrait of a woman holding in her lap a platter of fish. Set against what looked to her like fire—like the surface of the sun—the woman was featureless, or maybe it was that the fish she held was so intricately rendered on its platter of china blue, patterned round its rim with marine designs.

—I thought you didn't paint people.

—I don't, anymore.

Taking Isaac's hand she pulled him into her grin.

—Well, she said. If you don't paint me, don't paint anyone else.

The two paintings showed, academics would later suggest, a defiance of the subjective, or at least the human, the piscine forms on the rim of the dish hinting at the more abstract style he was beginning to adopt and which he maintained for what would, only years after his death, be called his career. When the paintings Kemper held that day were, as they say, rediscovered, along with the rest of his work in the mid-1960s, their provenance would contain no mention of this event and they were regarded as apprentice work and when brought up at auction fetched unremarkable sums.

They came out from the dim storeroom of the Museum of Art into the marble chill of the lobby and, passing between the milling people and the statues, went hand in hand down the granite steps that opened onto City Park, where they heard that the war in Europe had just begun.

It happened just after they joined a crowd watching acrobats negotiate the sky. A small show sprung up on the grass beside the peristyle. They stood with their heads tipped back, throats bared to the tightrope's line, which bowed with the weight of the man who walked it, a Hungarian whose name when he was not on the wire was Boldiscar Ujj, the soles of his feet folding over the braid while aerialists on either side cut flips, placing different hats on his head as they passed.

They kept close, drifting in the languages of the crowd, which was, in accordance with the law, made up entirely of persons considered white. As it happened, they thought little of this fact, of the black people on the periphery of their lives, that the world itself had been constructed like a picture garden whose turns showed a vantage meant for you alone. They were not, had it been put to them, indifferent, but they were blind as you might be to what lies beyond your sight. So they cheered with the crowd as the walker advanced to the center of the rope, when suddenly there came rivers of shouting boys with golfball biceps bunched over special editions of the papers; shouting the word that stood in bold type on the front page. The crowd fought for copies, the shape of the word flocking suddenly to Kemper and Isaac's eyes as all around them papers opened. And to the eye of Boldiscar Ujj on the rope. No net between him and the fluttering black wings of the world war. Unless the promoter insisted otherwise, he preferred to work free. A purveyor of astonishment, he kept walking even as war overtook the crowd and snatched away their awe, and he knew instantly, sure as the sun beat the back of his neck, that there could be no feat to equal this; he would never steal so much breath even if the next step he took was onto open air and he flew.

On the ground all was outcry. Kemper and Isaac, closer now, muttered in each other's ears, saying everything and nothing, their eyes, like those of all the people on the ground, fixed on the headlines and the details of the German advance into Belgium, so that few if any saw the tightrope walker fall.

In the hotel room, night leaning on the panes, they sat up awake trading roles the way people do when the world shifts on its axis. When the realization comes that everything has changed. For a while he'd be the one who was angry, then the one who said everything would be all right. All time, in the back of Kemper's mind, was the thought of what the next day meant for her. Of the stocks, the shares, her family. Like many children of wealth, she wanted her comfort without being too near the source of it.

—I don't know why I'm nervous, she said. People would kill for this. People have.

—You'll be all right?

—I'll only be here for another day. Then I'll be right behind you.

When Isaac's train arrived in Biloxi, talk of the storm had overtaken news of the war, and by the time he was mixing concrete in his brother's shop, the men there were saying the hurricane was angling their way. Landfall sometime in the next day or so. His brother had heard it from a tug captain, who'd heard it from the weather bureau in New Orleans, and so Isaac left the clouds of stone-dust and went to the pharmacist's next door and asked to use their telephone. After a long time of questions and switches, the gasp of lines gone dead, he was connected with the front desk of the Grunewald and left a message for Kemper, telling her to stay in New Orleans through the storm. He felt no better after he'd hung up and so asked the counterman for a Western Union form and sent much the same message this way. After he'd handed the slip over and paid for his words, after he'd returned to the shop and the cold smell of quicklime and the sound of grinding stone, he told himself he didn't need to worry. She would hear, the trains wouldn't run when the storm was close, and anyway she'd grown up with hurricanes as much as he had. So he comforted himself into the afternoon which saw him boarding the windows of the shop and being driven, in the first rain, to his parents' house, where he helped his father nail the shutters closed and his mother bring things to the second floor, her eyes following him up the stairs, her tight mouth underscoring some point she was making in her head. Though he'd been living in the studio out back since June, he hadn't seen them much at all. He saw this reflected in his mother's face, which had begun to show signs of age.

—What's wrong? he said.

—Nothing, she said. You just seem . . . different.

He mumbled something, her son, and she looked back at him over her shoulder from the head of the stairs. Having children, she realized, was like being at the edge of a cliff that opened on an expanse so high and vast and unknowable that it made you want to lie down on your stomach and cling to the earth.

Five

Kemper left the hotel not long after Isaac, going on foot across Canal, passing the offices of Cuyamel Fruit (one day to merge with their mutual rivals, United Fruit) heading uptown and into the business district and the offices of Gulf Shipping, a seven-story granite temple on the corner of Poydras and Carondelet.

She was met in the lobby by an eager male secretary, who led her upstairs, saying little, and looking at her even less. She wondered if he'd been ordered not to look. When she was younger she would be brought, ceremonially, to the offices a few times a year (on holidays and certain Fridays when her father wanted to take her to the races) but she had not been back from the time she was fifteen and didn't remember anyone she saw.

She signed the papers in the presence of an attorney and an accountant, neither of whom she knew, in a small boardroom at a table which the secretary equipped with a decanter of water and a blotter, wordlessly removing the ashtray embossed with the stylized waves of the company logo: an oval outlined in what looked like gunsmoke (and which was drawn as such in certain Latin American political cartoons) encompassing a stylized, forward-slanting wave. She listened to the statements of both men, sternly and without much comment, as she imagined the subject of such business must conduct herself. Though she knew from her childhood that real business consisted of nights spent pacing and muttering threats, of her mother's tears, her plucked nerves, and more than anything of fear—a fear she could never fully grasp, but which afflicts a great many men of business.

As she capped her pen, Red came into the boardroom wearing a suit that might have been one of his father's but for the cut of the lapels, his chin bearing a thick, pink scar so clear and clean against his skin she thought he might've given it to himself, the way she'd heard some young attorneys dyed their temples gray or in the old days wore false whiskers. A product of his desire to seem tested, hard, capable of violence. She rose from the table, not answering the murmured goodbyes of the men, and made her way to the door and Red who stood before it.

Her brother raised his hand and started to say, *Wait*, but she swept his hand away and shot out into the hall. In the instant that she passed him, she'd glimpsed something strange in his eyes, something caged, and it almost seemed like the next thing he was going to say was *Help*.

She put this away and hurried through the hall and into the mezzanine of that floor, which opened on the heart of the building, and down the next flight where, leaning at the railing, bent and gaunt, she found her father.

He said her name like a question and it was clear he didn't know why she was there. He turned to his daughter and she was so stunned by his thinness, by the gnarled shape of his back, that she immediately embraced him, what remained of him, frail under her fingers, and let him hold her arm as they walked from floor to floor, winding down the mezzanine, talking, until they reached the lobby where she, bitterly and for the last time, left him.

She took one of the last trains out of the city, which departed that afternoon with just under two hundred passengers in a driving rain and a headwind that blew up into a full gale by evening and made halting progress through the marshes to the northeast, nudging toward the coast. Nightfall came before its time, the lights in the cars raised, the mood among the passengers growing tenser with each stop, voices gone silent as the cars shuddered on the tracks. It was not yet the time when prayers were openly said, when the train would lurch to a halt, but looking out her rainwashed window as they crossed the Pointe aux Herbes and the track bent north so before the crossing at Chef Menteur Pass (one of the few justly named places in America—the nickname given by the Choctaw to a colonial governor, in honor of his frequent perfidy) she saw that the water surging into Lake Borgne was coming over the tracks.

—You look dark, her father had said. Your neck looks like a country girl's.

This had been when they were walking down the mezzanine together, circling the chandelier and its gold-leaf fount of bursting fruits, crystal dripping from its arms. Below them a sea of voices.

She smiled at him. —What do you know about the country, she said.

—Not much, thank God, he said. There's nothing more stupid and Southern than a millionaire talking about fields and fatback and cornbread.

She told him she couldn't stay, but her father didn't seem to hear. He went on talking, and she felt the part of herself she'd barred from him open, just a bit. She recognized in him the things she loved. He was not one those soft fathers, always cooing over his little girl (he did not even like when she would sometimes call him Daddy), nor one wracked with nightmares over his daughter's virginity (he regarded the social mores of his class as he did all such institutions and persons who did not serve his immediate needs, with contempt), nor one of those fathers who recuse themselves from the lives of their daughters out of sheer dismay that they had produced one of the very creatures who'd bedeviled them into the act of conception in the first place (for he was raised by women and, for all his bluster, was more comfortable in their company than that of other men).

He said she should visit her mother and Kemper gave his arm a pat.

—You should do the same, she said.

—My mother died forty years ago, he said. I was at her bedside with her, when there was almost no one left in the city. Eighteen seventy-eight. The worst fever in a generation. Bodies in yards, wherever they fell. Barrels of creosote. I sent your mother and you children off, but I stayed. I was right there with her for almost a month, burning sulfur (the doctors said it did something or another) and mixing washtubs with bichloride of mercury to disinfect her clothes, her sheets. She hated that; it was bad for the fabric. There she was, laid out dying, furious over those ruined dresses. But I suppose your mother was furious too, with me for staying, for having to take you all.

—I wasn't alive then, Dad, Kemper said.

But he didn't seem to hear and went on talking about how he'd made plans to strip the wallpaper from his mother's house, he was so sure she would live, telling Kemper about the house itself, the little place on Kerlerec where they'd moved in the third year of the war and where he and Marina had done the last of their growing up together. How small it was, how many pounds of sulfur you had to burn per room. Nine pounds! he said. Think about that.

—Finally my mother said to me, Baby I'd rather die than smell that anymore. She wanted rosewater and hibiscus. Bay lime. She hadn't called me "baby" in years. So I kept on with the sulfur and medicine but she kept getting weaker and weaker, weaker than I knew possible. She'd never once been weak. A weak woman couldn't have gotten us through my father's death and what came after, couldn't have buried one man and killed another, or have it done, in the span of a year at the age of thirty-four. But she was so weak then I had to help her on and off the pot, which is a thing to do, I can tell you, lifting your mother like that.

—You never told me this before, she said.

Her father stopped.

—Why would I have, he said.

She didn't know, couldn't say. They were two floors from the street and you could see the carts and trucks passing in the windows, goods hurtling through the first of the rain.

—It's funny, he said, turning to Kemper. There was a lot of help from the North then. Piles and piles of clothes sent down from New York. I read about the drives later, the people lining up on Broadway feeling good about themselves. He laughed: When it was all over and they reopened the river in late November, when my mother and God knows how many people were dead, the city of St. Louis sent down a pair of relief boats. Nothing had come into New Orleans for months. And I remember standing at the landing, waiting for those ships, alone. They unloaded four tons of ice and crates of canned food and, I'll never forget, fifteen hundred bottles of champagne, two hundred gallons of whiskey, and four hundred cases of Budweiser beer. I'd buried her that morning.

Word passed from car to car, by porters and passengers, that the keeper of the bridge ahead had refused to raise the draw for oncoming ships and abandoned his post some hours earlier. Now the pylons were snarled with wrecked schooners and lugs, those who'd aimed to ride out the storm and whose crews had climbed the legs of the bridge and now clung to the trestle and the tracks.

Not long after the news came to Kemper's car, so too did a sailor, limp and soaked, carried by passengers from the front and laid out across a row of seats near her aisle. Towels and blankets were found in a porter's hutch and the man was being bandaged and dried when the car began to shudder with the waves and the train jerked into motion again. Unbeknownst to them, the engineer had decided to try to cross the pass and get as far as they could from the open water, into the marsh where the waves would be broken. When Kemper pressed her cheek to the window, straining to see ahead, she saw the forward cars moving through the waves.

They made it as far as Bay St. Louis, where the waves had torn the tracks away and, in the same way they'd heard about the bridge, the passengers got word that the train would go no farther. They would be here for whatever was to come.

—Is Marina sick? she'd said to her father when they'd come to the ground floor.

—You think that's why I'm telling you this?

Kemper shrugged.

—Well, I wouldn't know if she was, he said, his faint voice wandering in the desert of his throat. Her father stopped to catch his breath and when he had it asked if she'd seen Red.

—I don't have anything to say to him, she said.

—So he hasn't told you.

—What?

Later she would tell herself that she'd done the right thing by staying, hearing him out. Every word of the whole rotten thing until her father stopped and all that lay between them was silence, golden fruit, and crystal light. He told her that her brother, Angel, was dead.

—Where?

—In Nicaragua. Killed in the fighting. One of their damn wars.

—How long have you known?

—We've . . . we heard things, but couldn't be sure. Now—

—How long?

His face bent into a scowl. —A year, almost two.

No words came to her then, no expression for this hurt. He was saying they'd only heard rumors, didn't know for sure, that he didn't want to tell her, God, much less her mother, until he knew for certain. He stared up at her, shrinking. In a moment she would go past him into the lobby and there would be the secretary, the car, the train, the storm. She couldn't bring herself to speak, but she could and did take her father's hands for a moment, before she let him go.

This man, so fragile now, saying this wasn't how he wanted it to be.

The roar of wind then, and the cars rocking and the marsh around them an unbroken sheet of rushing water. The voices of the people near her rising as they made frantic gambler's negotiations with their god or wept or talked, aimless words, bouncing children on their knees or holding the hand of the person next to them. The windows lit of a sudden and great legs of lightning raced over the water. Kemper made her way up the aisle, holding a lost child of indefinite sex. The car was shaking, and as she held the squirming child she thought of the house on Deer Island, torn apart and flung in fragments across the Gulf, objects of her childhood summers swept south by currents to wash up in Cuba for her mother to find. It did not matter that her mother lived a good distance from the coast; Kemper imagined the people with wings coming down from their mountain hidingplaces to the beach and picking up the dish or dress or water-logged sheet music and, flying inland, depositing them on her mother's doorstep. When the sky went bright again the child had broken free and Kemper fell into the next seat she could find. The car shook. It was just past midnight.

Around this time the house on Deer Island was taken apart. The water unseated the foundation, broke down doors; the wind snatched tiles from the roof and then the boards beneath, bursting windows and tearing, finally, the whole roof away so that the house lay hollow as a bleached skull. By morning all that remained were three walls belted with dark mud and seaweed, as Isaac saw when he rowed from his parents' house, which had luckily only taken on a foot or so of water, across to Biloxi. There he heard from fishermen who'd ridden out the storm on their boats that a train from New Orleans had been trapped on the trestle not far past Bay St. Louis. Seeing him grow pale, and because they were heading out that way to check on cousins and assess the damage done (and salvage what they could from ships wrecked in the marsh, though none mentioned this), the fishermen agreed to take him along as a hand. So at eight that morning he was aboard a croaking shrimper that smelled of iodine and from which dried scales fluttered in the air as they motored up the coast, dodging rafts of flotsam, the men turning to point at various wonders. A drowned cow. A sailboat in the treetops off Pass Christian.

Isaac at the gunnels, holding on to hope.

The first boats that came upon the stalled train were pirogues poled by boys from a rat's nest settlement in the marsh, their families the owners of a clapboard store that had yet to turn a profit. Upon seeing them, the passengers hung out the traincar windows, poured onto the tracks, shouting, waving handkerchiefs. The boats were too small to take on any refugees and besides they had no way of getting the stranded people down. Instead, the boys sold them bottled drinks at an enormous premium, and most were too stunned and thirsty to balk. So by means of a basket lowered by knotted sheets from the sleeping car the exchange was made and the clearing day saw Kemper sitting on the tracks, legs dangling free, sipping a warm Grapico she'd uncapped on the head of a spike. She heard the shouts from farther on that a boat was coming alongside. She smiled, flush with life, and watched as the passengers rushed to the edge of the tracks. Bodies so tight-packed she couldn't see the boat as it neared or that from it leapt a man who scrambled up the trestle leg and shoved through the people on the tracks, calling something out. And it was only when he was almost on top of her that she believed it was his voice, her name.

PART 4

False Blue Sky

1915 – 1917

One

They moved so quickly then, like those creatures whose lives are gone in one beautiful, unbroken rush, hurrying before tomorrow finds them. Like the pale moths that returned each spring or the locusts' summer-long outcry that prefaces a sixteen-year silence, without dread or desperation but with purpose written in their blood. So fast that, when Isaac looked back, it would seem all one swift motion. A breathless sprint that lasted three years, the best, they would agree, of their lives. Neither would confess this to the other, though both knew it to be true. Much later, when flashes of that time lit the darkness of his old age, he would see her again, as she was in that season.

A time of nevers: She had never held a duckling, never gathered eggs. Never knelt by seedbeds or the nest of a tern. Never shared a bed for longer than a night or fallen asleep with a body close to hers full with the knowledge that it would be there when she woke. Never organized a house of her own. Never, she realized, felt loved, much less the sole focus of a love that leapt and burned into hours of exhaustion. Never known the wonder of saying what you wanted and having this other so willing to give or try; never felt so powerful and yet so afraid as then, when he was hers and even a cross word, much less a fight, could stun him into silence or fill his eyes with tears. Never known a tongue inside her or the taste of semen, just as he had never known the taste of himself mingled with another or the iron mystery of menstrual blood. He'd never been so free, so gone from the world, as though she'd stolen him away. Never known what it meant to truly need, all consequence channeled into one other person. And they grew each with their discoveries as nevers became known and they built their life, a wall that shut out a world which, in the years leading up to their country's entry into the Great War, was increasingly bent on destroying itself.

They bought a runabout Packard I-38 from a dealer in New Orleans whose family name Kemper recognized from her grandfather's book, a name that formerly hung over the city's most extensive slave-pens. She loved the car, all gleaming brass and whitewall tire, the roar of its six cylinders, but Isaac, horrified already by the cost, which was more than their house, more than his parents' house, shied from it like a dog at a loud noise, so they bought a bicycle too, which he rode to Biloxi where he still did occasional work for his brother. And as it happens in the country, they came into a menagerie of fowl: hens and guineas, red-faced Muscovy ducks that fought like drunks and roosted in the trees and rooted for insects in the dirt and leaves scattered beneath the underpinnings of their house.

The house had belonged to a once-prosperous German family, owners of a sawmill some miles inland, who had gone bust and left their land and business to the bank, seeking their fortunes elsewhere. The house had stood vacant for three years before Kemper and Isaac, who had planned for a more distant move after their wedding, found it on a ride and fell immediately in love with the place and, more, the land it stood on. Sited six miles down the coast from his parents' house, the property ran one acre wide and three deep. The land was cut out of old French arpents, bordered east and west by a V of creeks which fed into the bay, and to the north by the remains of a sawmill. Beyond was only an ugly stretch of stumps, sawgrass, and bayonet palm. But the Germans had chosen a fine place shielded from their work, and the trees there were spreading oaks and slash pine, and maple, which also served to screen the property from the lone road that passed nearby, accessible only by a shaded path of oystershell. In the shadows of the trees grew moss that held green for most of the year and spread in a carpet between the main house and the shed where the Germans had kept their adolescent sons and which Isaac converted to his studio.

November saw them take possession of the place and brought days of dust and rags and housepaint. They rode into town and bought a bucket of blue Climatic, and the next morning Isaac set about painting the ceilings of both porches. On the ride he'd started to explain the significance of the paint, but Kemper knew already. Said, I'm from here too, you know. Flies and ill-intentioned ghosts, mistaking the blue for the true sky, would rise upwards and miss the door. She knew this, and just as she knew that neither of them believed in spirits, nevertheless she was comforted by the blue sky overhead and the idea that the past could be confounded, turned away.

He woke her in the mornings when it was still dark, before he would go out on the water, because he couldn't stand the thought of her waking alone. She would come awake the same way each day, or so he would remember it, her arms curled at her sides, hands reaching out, while he spoke to her, saying where he'd go and when he would be back. As she fell back asleep he would dress and gather his things and take the boat out from the dock he'd built at the mouth of the creek, rowing as the sun rose, and daylight would find him beached on one of the barrier islands, lying in the lee of a dune, sketching, or waist-deep in a marshy pond making studies with the watercolors he'd lately adopted, painting on pasted sheets of typing paper held in a clipboard, cleaning the tip of his brush in the water at his hip, the colors draining into the colors of the world. He would return around midday and in his studio pin the detailed studies and the sketches to a clothesline, and these images would reappear on canvases in careful strokes forming the illusion of an unbroken motion.

They made trips to New Orleans in the runabout and returned with the backseat filled with bolts of canvas and other art supplies, with things she missed like loaves of bread or good sausage, and especially bottles of whiskey and wine (unavailable in dry Mississippi), which lent trips a criminal tinge, and they joked, over the roaring engine, of being on the run. More often than not Isaac seemed glad to go, but he had to be convinced to attend the opening of the exhibition at the Museum of Art. He refused for a week leading up to the event, retreating into himself, and, when she pressed him, gave increasingly frantic reasons why they shouldn't go. She tried her best to be gentle, but it didn't matter, and one night in late December, when she asked again, he was on the verge of panic. A different person, or rather a person burrowed deep in the one she knew.

She saw the fear in his eyes, heard it in his voice, learned its timbre and the signs of its arrival: his sudden need to flee or to never move (which itself was a form of flight), the self-sabotage. The strange, almost petty refusal to acknowledge his own work in public, she would come to understand, was as much a part of him as was the art. At first she thought it nothing more than ego or the fear of being criticized, but then she saw it came from a darker place than that. Like a child's wince at an upraised hand. She would fight against this burrowed self for as long as they were together, always the one who fought and soothed and urged when the fear or whatever it was had him. And even though she was not one of those indomitable props for an ever-faltering man, and even though these times were tortuous, she would go on fighting it, hating the responsibility his panic placed on her, but then there were times more numerous and true that she saw him overcome, paralyzed, and weak, and she hoped that what she did, urging him out, was slowly, drop-by-drop, changing him for the better.

◆ ◆ ◆

She did, finally, convince him to attend the opening. They arrived hours late, dashing up the museum steps with the night of City Park singing all around them, the Packard parked aslant. Then, and to her great surprise, his panic fled. Maybe it was relief, or maybe the presence of his parents, who hugged him and then kept a beaming distance for the rest of the night, but he was happy. Taking Kemper's arm, Isaac led her through the gallery, pointing out details in others' work, got a little drunk but didn't rant or sneer, let alone tear down canvases or challenge another painter to a fight (all of which she imagined to be commonplace at art events, which she quickly discovered were in fact muted, nervy affairs). He introduced her to people he knew and she saw how they brightened in his presence, and in a way it was like watching sparks of her own love floating round him. One of them, a painter called Guillory, whose work was not on display, clung to them early on and stayed stuck until the end of the night. He and Isaac had been students together in the class of a New Orleans tutor years before but their paths had diverged radically from there (no eastern art school for Guillory, who painted portraits and nursery walls for money), crossing only at such events. Guillory's latest project, he said, was a cycle called *The Suffragettes*, nudes and voluptuaries in the Pre-Raphaelite mold, but each of them in some way defaced. He used his shaving razor, he used paint, he used liniment, he used a brick, a garden trowel. So far he had four mauled beauties.

—Why? Kemper said.

—Up in London they're defacing paintings by the dozen, the suffragettes are. Anything too saucy and they're on it with claws and cleavers.

Kemper, who'd done some suffrage work herself, at least up to the point of attending lectures, laughed as Guillory went on:

—They say they want to draw attention to how women are portrayed, are *seen*, but that's just focusing on the object. What I'm concerned with is the subject.

Isaac listened as Guillory went on describing his series, watched Kemper nod and laugh at the appropriate times, and felt cold clenching fingers of a familiar guilt—for the wasted education and the connections to eastern art circles thrown away, and, more, that despite his failure he'd been given a place here in the exhibition, and that Guillory, whose work excited and troubled him, had not.

Just before the end of the night Isaac was approached by the owner of a new gallery in the Quarter, a small man dressed as though he were clinging desperately to a new social height and who, handing Isaac a flute of champagne, told him exactly what he wanted to hear about his work. The gallery owner talked about a solo show in the spring, and Isaac hastily agreed, seeing over the little man's shoulder both Kemper and Guillory listening. Guilt and triumph like mating hawks soaring and falling together inside him.

At the end of the night the three of them—Kemper, Isaac, and Guillory—celebrated in the only open café they could find nearby. A German place, a kind of brasserie with ranks of small iron tables crowded with others their age as well as dancers draped with overcoats like hastily wrapped parcels and old men in eveningwear paired in debate or the solitary contemplation of a coffee cup. Overhead a dozen wicker ceiling fans whirred. They found a place near the long cypress bar where, past the taps, three men who looked like brothers shucked oysters and set the halves in a bed of steaming ice. They drank lagers, tooth-cracking cold, which had been brewed in cypress tanks so that the beer had the faint taste of a fall breeze at the edge of a bayou and was perfect with the oysters and the chilled shrimp they ordered. They tipped oysters back and drank and talked, smoking all of Guillory's cigarettes. When the subject of her family came up, Kemper was not so much surprised that Guillory knew who they were but that he was so forward about it.

—So, he said, is the rumor true?

—Which one? she said, lifting an eyebrow as Isaac laughed.

—Oh, that you're secret blacks, Guillory said quickly and half under his breath.

Now it was her turn to laugh, the beer softening what would normally be annoyance.

—Every family in New Orleans says that about every other family, she said, if they're pissed or jealous enough.

—That's true, Guillory conceded. Everyone's worried that if they tap their toe too much to a band on the streetcorner they'll be—whoosh—transported straight back to darkest Africa. Undone. He leaned to Isaac. So what do you think?

—I'm not much on family histories, he said.

—If you must know, Kemper said to Guillory, it is true.

Guillory's eyes widened, straining to maintain the urbane look of a savorer of scandals.

Kemper drew on her cigarette and the smoke bit the back of her throat. She'd had this conversation, or versions of it, before. Mostly with Angel, who, out of all her family, was the one who felt as she did about this truth. That it was meaningless, fractions cribbed by mad people of a madder time. The fact laid bare in the pages of their grandfather's (the first Angel Woolsack's) book, the gist being that their grandmother was however-many-parts-per-hundred black, a descendent of those who'd fled what became Haiti at the beginning of the nineteenth century. The numbers, which had been belabored for the first Angel Woolsack when he made plans to take a young wife in his later years, were so trivial, so faint, the notations of a chemistry experiment. The fact was also that after the suicide of the first Angel Woolsack, in the legal wrangling over his estate, the young wife had sued, been countersued, and ultimately won a case in court that declared her legally both white and wealthy, which meant free. Kemper's mother had told her this, mistaking the girl's curiosity for fear. Like her brother Angel, she saw in this fleck of family history none of the menace others did, who feared secrets like cancerous growths which might at any time turn on their host. And when Kemper saw the fear manifested in others or in books (where it was given much store, the lynchpin ruin of proud, aristocratic lines) it struck her as absurd. Certainly it mattered more if it showed in the skin, or maybe if you labored under the delusion that your family line was an otherwise sunlit path strolled by diligent, happy (and thus white) forebears. But in an ocean of so much blood, how could this drop matter except, she thought, as guilt made manifest. Then it seemed even more a conceit. So that to Kemper people like her brother Red, who was haunted by the blood, seemed less a person than an actor struggling with a role. Whenever it had come up between the siblings, it was Red who smarted, who, though he treated as gospel the words of his crazed grandfather, chose to deny, to the point of rage and tears, the few lines that dwelled on this revelation. She could see him now, sweating as he pored over some fashionable current book on racial hierarchies. And this pleased her.

—The thing is, she told Guillory, that's far from the worst secret we have.

She proceeded to relate a series of killings, revolutions, thefts, usurpations, and iniquities that ran the better part of a century, like someone reading the rise and fall of stocks or the results of horseraces from a rapidly unspooling ticker, until her cigarette was gone and Guillory was shifting uncomfortably in his chair and Isaac put his hand to her thigh, wanting her to stop. He hated these moments, when she sank into her family, punishing herself. Weighing herself down over and again with guilt that wasn't hers, or shouldn't be. Whenever she spoke to him of her family, even the brother she loved, he imagined them as figures of cold, sharp stone, with Kemper the lone warm, living thing at their heart. Why, he wondered, did people love dragging out all the bad that had come before them? The same as how country people who rise above their station will joke with others who have done the same about how much their daddies and mamas beat them. What was it for, this continual unearthing, the worrying of the same wounds?

Then she was talking about her oldest brother, the one who was dead. She was telling stories that were still meant to shock, things he'd done, stories of mercenaries and deposed presidents, but Isaac could hear the notes of sadness creeping into her voice. He knew she would pay for this later, when they were alone and her guilt would rear its head, the waves of blame gnawing at her heart and the empty space where Angel's death should've been.

The sun was out when they left the café, promising to see Guillory again soon and have him out to the house. They drove back through morning, heads clearing in the wind, stopping at a deserted stretch of beach where they lay out, talking. About Isaac's luck, about Guillory, who they would see a few more times before he joined the French Army, claiming familial ties, and whose death they would read about in the paper. They bathed in the cold water, jolting their headaches loose. Kemper felt the city peeling from her skin and looked to Isaac, who'd swum out to a sandbar and was bent, stomach lined in little ridges, splashing his face. He seemed so at home. So right, here.

By mid-February he'd finished *Tiger Shark and Lovers* and was at work on a series he thought of as *The Nests* but which would ultimately be renamed at the suggestion of the owner of the Gallery Delpit, who saw them when he visited during the Mardi Gras holidays.

Then it was the season of birds, the islands filling with chattering hordes of migrants building nests of sticks and reeds fixed with their glue-like spit or furrowed in the sand in a patch of sea oat. His series were close visions of these works, the colors of the eggs of gallinules and terns like shadows on the hashwork of the nests. In the afternoons, when he was finished, Kemper might go out with him on the boat, to fish, or to one of the islands where they would drink, eat, fuck, and watch flocks of thousands enact variations of the same. This was the only season in which she would accompany him to the islands, preferring the chill and the wind and the birds to the swarming insects of summer. She liked it now, at the start of the year, walking the beach, hearing the great clamor of the birds on the windward side like a coming storm. A vast, loud presence that made you feel insignificant though it couldn't hurt you, like the rain on the tin roof of their house and the wonderful deep sleeps it brought.

But all loves have their dark corners, and if his was panic and isolation, hers was this: Like her country, she didn't know what to do with peace. She might enjoy it for a time, but always at hand was rage, which only grows less explicable in disuse. Urgent as air when you're holding your breath, the emotion that had served her well in her time of growing up, that bound her to her kin, was there, waiting. So she got too drunk with him and the anger would return to her. No slow gathering of hurts, the traditional squabbles and resentments, these outbursts were spontaneous and when they held her there was nothing he could do. Nothing he *would* do—his passivity driving her to further heights of fury as (she later realized) she tried to urge the same rage out of him. He would be crying, clawing at himself, trying to find something to be sorry for, which there often was but not to scale with her anger. He would remember each time he felt the sickening release of fighting back, confirming to her every awful thing she suspected about herself and which, perversely, she wanted proven. You are cruel. You are spoiled. Then he would feel more shattered than if he'd said nothing at all. He began to think of these times as visitations of her family ghosts, the past she both wanted to own and be absolved from. And a part of him wanted them, the rages, longed for the hours they would spend in bed afterwards, whole days of healing. Then, as it happens, the healing overtook the rages and the outbursts grew fewer and farther between. Of course, we're never rid of darkness, and she'd suffer from bouts now and then over the next few years, before he was taken from her, and when they came and she could find no word or action to relieve them, Kemper would go out into the yard and he would hear a sound not unlike that of a panther—not a wounded call, but a sound that claimed the space in which it could be heard, a cry given back to all the others that rose up to surround them of a night, when the voices of the creatures in the reeds, the grasses, and the trees joined like pieces of a wall, and he alone on the porch or adding kindling to the fire in the range would hear her calling out to everything.

"*. . . and she began to learn the life of the coast.*"

A line Kemper found in a novel that she borrowed from Isaac's mother, who read for illumination and instruction, keeping little sheets of notes and underlining passages she liked. For his mother, books existed as companions, enriching reality. Kemper thought of her own mother, who loved books as descents, surrenders, and was herself freer in the suspension of reality than when she was forced, by a child's tugging hand perhaps, to rejoin the waking life. Kemper remembered how her mother would (and likely still did) blink and stare when she was forced to look up from whatever pages she had at hand, like an intended suicide hauled from the water by well-meaning strangers. Kemper read the line in the novel, which was not marked or underscored, over and again, and felt it was a sign, something meant for her. She read it aloud to Isaac and would say it sometimes, unbidden, like a chant—when they were on the water and the green back of a sea turtle swept past, or when the surf was roiling phosphorescence, or a swarm of sea life flopped and crawled onto their shore at the sign of certain moons, when the strangeness of the wild, everything new and yet unimaginably old, overwhelmed her. And she began.

Two

The Gallery Delpit, where Isaac's solo show was held in April 1917, was located at the edge of the Quarter in the shabby first floor of a building whose upper stories housed a miracle cure concern. The smell of sour herbs bitter as false hope wafted down through cracks in the ceiling, giving everyone light heads. Kemper held Isaac's arm (it had taken a week to work him out of his panic, and she had suffered many weeks before that of mania and doubt as he finished his series), watching as the light of attention fled him as the guests—his parents, game as ever, some old teachers—petered out and the wine was gone, and by the end of the night he was like a burnt-out filament beside her. What he still thought of as *The Nests* hung together on one wall, the individual pieces opposite, all unsold.

Money was the least of this. The shares she'd come into at the age of twenty-one, whose yield Kemper had diverted into stocks, assured they would be free to live however they liked. And she kept to herself the dread that all the joy of their idle, beautiful life together, every loveliness she found in the tasks of their day—washing eggs at the pump or laying bedding for the birds—existed only because of the money. That if they had to do these things in order to survive, that if, like their neighbors, there was consequence pulsing in the stalk of each plant, in the red heart of each egg, then necessity would grind joy down to dust. She didn't share with him the typed reports she received twice a year from an attorney in New Orleans, her proxy in all dealings as a shareholder in Gulf Shipping, and the guilt, which was of course not strong enough to make her give the money up. It held her as it did all her family, like the gravity of the world the money gave them.

Around this time there was a spate of articles about groups of children who shared the same dreams. Sometimes, she read, the children were found to be half siblings, the products of secret infidelities, but more often no relationship could be determined other than, say, attending the same school, and the mystery of the communal dreams sank into the backpages of the newspapers, unable to hold a public imagination gripped by news of the war. And was the war, which her country now eyed hungrily, the dream or the waking? You heard talk then of renaming streets, villages called Germantown became Washington or Lincoln overnight, things that seemed silly at first, but then there were beatings and the formations of patriot groups that sought to root out dissent as ugliness and outrage went from something that happened elsewhere to a fact of daily life, and the German café where she and Isaac had eaten with Guillory had its windows broken, and vaguely Teutonic families were evicted from their homes. You heard of a young man in Tennessee who cut off his hand in order to avoid conscription and who had bled out and died. You heard old women speaking outside the dentist's office in Biloxi, saying how the man inside was doing a right smart business now that some boys had heard a soldier was required to have a full set of back teeth. You tried not to hear or see young men in fits of patriotism beating other young men, without molars perhaps, and the drills and parades and endless brass-throated music. But, for better or worse, the South was still a touch suspicious of the war, if only that it would enrich the industrial North. Among the six senators who voted against entering the war and against the Selective Service Act was one James K. Vardaman of Mississippi, who publicly pledged that if maintaining white supremacy meant lynching every negro in his state, he'd have it done, and as governor once choked half to death an inmate of the state farm then serving as a butler in his mansion. The senator's decision against bloodshed on a global scale, though his own state was ruled by bloodshed on a scale of centuries, was as dry an irony as the fact that the beaten, strangled inmate went on to save Governor Vardaman's life when the latter rode in to quell a riot at the prison. When she read of the vote, Kemper would wonder whether these were lights in the near universal darkness of the history of the state or merely a deepening of the dark. A darkness they were, inescapably, a part of. The war abroad, which was coming, and the war at home, which they and so many others had put out of their minds, hiding behind art and beauty. They were young and white and had money, and this combination could put you a good ways out of the path of the world's great reaping. But not in every case. She read the editorials of the dissenters, which were printed less and less, until the signing of the Espionage Act, when dissent disappeared entirely from the papers, replaced by accounts of valor and the numbers of the dead. She read the news aloud to Isaac, who would stare blankly into the middle distance or get up and walk down from the porch into the yard. For a while they comforted themselves with lies, but only for a while. You tell yourself a terrible change has come over your country and that everything is different, then you wake one day and realize you're living in the country as it's always been.

That spring Isaac discovered a small grove of red mulberry at the rear of the property, planted by some distant husbandman who must have dreamed of silk, and which in early spring had grown berries pale green as geckos' bellies which ripened after the rain and became a beacon to cowbirds, blackbirds, thrashers. The berries so ripe they rained down from the negligible weight of the hollow-boned, winged bodies that lit in the branches or with the brush of your hands, as they did when Isaac led her there one evening not long after he received the order to register for the draft. Within the tree and the leaves flecked with purple birdshit they ate the berries and the tender green stems that clung to them until their hands were gloved, their mouths purple smears. They sat together as the night came alive.

He told her about something he'd seen in the Yucatán, when he'd hiked out of Santa Elena, trying to find the Kabah gate. He hadn't found the ruins, but after a week caught a ride back on a truck owned by International Harvester, which took him through the fields of henequen. The spined arms of the henequen plant hacked by men in rags who were themselves flogged with watered ropes by other men. It made no difference that the men who held the ropes were Korean (so he learned from the driver) and the men being whipped were Mayan or Yaqui; what he saw then was the history of his homeland, the passing of the whip from one hand to another, and whether someone held the whip for you or you held it yourself was meaningless. He'd looked away, here in Mississippi, as much as he could. But now they were holding out the whip and saying, It's your turn.

—I won't be a part of it, he said. I won't go die for that.

She said that she would be with him, that he was brave. But he didn't sound brave. He sounded very much afraid, as was she.

In the morning she would find their traces, winepress footprints on the porch steps, leading back to the house. The shapes of their feet alive with sugar ants. The stains would not lift until the third flood of that summer, so that his path was there, visible to her when she looked out from the kitchen window, even after he was gone.

January 1919
S.S. *Sud*

Sister,

Now that you know that I'm alive, maybe the next thing you should know is how I died.

    I left Nicaragua two weeks ago, and it's been days since I last slept. In the pitch and roll of the Pacific I could close my eyes and almost be gone, but now that the ship has crossed the isthmus and come into the calm, I can't even do that. Nights I pace the deck with an antique pistol in my pocket. I watch the men on their watches smoking cigarettes and staring out at what for me is only emptiness, a distance to be crossed, but for them is something filled with possibility. Spaces and silences are like that. Certain eyes can see in them, certain hearts wish to.

You're one of those people, I think, little sister. You wrote me for years, sending out messages across the space of my silence. I could lie and say I never got your letters, but I did. Most of them. I read them in batches, little bundles every few weeks, sometimes longer, and I can trace down to the month how long it took for you to finally give me up. How the letters grew less and less frequent until they finally stopped. I waited for that time the way you wait for a loved one at the edge of death to pass over, a hope with guilt at its heart. A hope I know too well now, like so many others in the world. When the first month went by with no word from you I was glad, glad for you but also because your silence balanced mine out. So I began to imagine you, what happened in your silence, just like you must have imagined me, even after you heard I was dead.

It happened like this. On the night of 4 October 1912, though my body wouldn't be found until the next morning by a detachment of U.S. Marines—a corpse with a ruined face crumpled behind the Church of Our Lady of the Assumption in the town of Masaya, in Nicaragua. A pretty town of weavers and craftsmen, canopies of citrus, grass growing in the road, or at least it was before the shelling. I doubt they were surprised to find me, the Marines. They know as well as you or I how wars in the center and south of the Americas tend to be salted with North American corpses. Because when you're a country that's bound to the United States, as Nicaragua is, with Wall Street owning the measure of her imports and exports and indebted from here to doomsday, it means not only that you're chained to a monumental, munificent b—h, but that you're bound to suffer her wayward children too. I like to imagine that once I was identified by the papers in my pocket the Marines tossed the body into the oxcart they used to drag the corpse of our last general, Benjamín Zeledón, down the Catalina road to his burial farther south. People tell me it was a sight. The Marines trotting their horses, the General's head lolling.

The General had been killed sometime in the night, at the fortress of the Coyotepe, some miles north of the town. We knew he was dead and that the fort had fallen when shells started to fall and the guns of the fort across the gorge turned on us in Masaya. Now Masaya had seen fire before. There is, or was, an icon of San Jerónimo there that some priest a century ago, when the volcano woke, had taken out and marched with at the head of his congregation to face down the fireballs and clastic flows. Imagine that, believing that you can stand before a mountain or fire and will it to stop. Our grandfather was like that, our father was like that, and there is some of that in us. The stupidity to believe that the impossible is something you can do, and the wildness to try. The icon, charred by some spat volcanic rock, was kept in the church near where the boy was found. Now it's all burnt, and that night, when it was clear we had lost, I was sitting in the barroom of the Hotel Ascarate, just across the plaza from the church of the burnt saint, and drinking, not alone.

In the years since I left you, four men have come looking for and found me. The first I paid off, the second I lost, the third I killed in British Honduras. My conscience is untroubled, at least on these counts. The fourth was sitting across from me in the hotel barroom, sipping from a dented pewter flask while the bombs shook sheets of plaster from the walls and you could hear the roof tiles shatter in the square.

He was, the fourth man, my age and American. Said he was an attorney from Mobile, Alabama, though he lived in Nicaragua now. Said his name was Jefferson Davis Edwards and that today was his lucky day. I'd seen him lurking around the hotel for days, but thought little of him, believing he was one of those salt grains I mentioned earlier, until that night when he stepped into the bar and strode over to where I was and sat down like he'd been invited.

The shells were coming more and more now. The whole hotel shook, and the door that led out onto the plaza hung by a half-broken hinge.

"Mr. Woolsack," he said, laughing like people do when they come finally to some much-discussed monument, something you just have to see.

I told him he was wrong, but he grinned and said he had proof. Took from some inner pocket of his soiled jacket an enlarged print of a snapshot taken many years ago, in my early twenties. Our father paid for it, as I recall, the original on the table beside our mother's bed. The man smoothed out the creases and slid the photo across the table, and then I was facing my own face. Or what used to be mine.

"So," I said. "What happened to him?"

"He vanished, about two years ago."

"Vanished," I said, liking the sound of the word.

"Ordinary people are abandoned, taken, killed, even lost," he said. "But people of property, the sons and daughters of money, they vanish. *Poof.* And their families look and look, or if they're like most rich families, all squabbling over who gets what money, they have these vanished persons declared dead so they can cash out indemnities taken out on that life when that life was much newer. But the Mutual Insurance and Indemnity Corp., and some other interested parties, believe it is within what's called the 'balance of possibility' that you, Angel Woolsack, are alive."

"And you came here in the middle of a war to find out."

"Shit," he said. "There's always a war. You should know that better than anybody. Far as I can tell you've been present at every bloodletting this place has seen since you were about eighteen years old."

"I'm an investor," I said. "I'm here overseeing my investments."

"I don't doubt it. You just invested in the wrong side this time."

At that moment some officers came down the gallery bearing crates and bags and, between two of them, an enormous Gilder typewriter, which they hefted onto the bar while one officer found a bottle and they passed it back and forth. They saw me sitting there, saw that something was wrong, but I gave them a look that said, Go on, don't worry about me.

It seemed like the shells were falling just outside the door, which somehow still hung on. Dust and smoke and pieces of stone wafting in, the breath of bombs.

"I don't blame you," the Alabaman said. "I came here to vanish too. It's not much different from home: Same bugs. Same heat. Minus the language. Minus the wars. Minus the mountains. Different niggers, though, don't you find? Down on the coast they like white folks, hate 'de Sponish.'" He laughed. "Then you got these men coming down from California talkin' 'greaser' this and 'spic' that, but if you're from the South it's like home or better—a home where no one knows you."

For a moment I thought of saying something true, but there's a point in the life of many a white Southerner, maybe it's come to you, when you're so sick of disabusing your piss-ignorant countrymen of their more closely-held notions that you just quit and get up and take your chances with whatever the hell is outside.

So I did. I stood with my bag and of course so did the man, so that I saw the grip of the pistol at his side.

"You want to tip the balance of possibility," I asked.

The Alabaman's face brightened. "To be honest," he said, "I don't care if Mutual pays out. They paid me to make a report, and I've already sent it. For them, you're officially, as of three days ago, alive and in this town. But to the United Fruit Company, who you have flat out egregiously f—d for almost a decade, it matters quite a bit."

I remember how he said it and the change that passed over his face. And I wonder what he saw in mine at that moment. Did he see what I was willing to do? What I would do without a second thought, because I might be better than some in our family but I still have that gap in me where care should be about ending the life of someone in your way. But before I could, a shell hit the front of the hotel and everything was smoke and splinters.

You told me once that you hoped we were happy, meaning me and whoever I loved. I know from your letters that you and the man you love have been happy, or were, and that's good. Why is it easier for me to write the second sentence than the first? Now that the war they say will be the last is done and the 'flu is finished with us, what took a clear quarter of the world, and the quarantines are lifted and I am freed by the awful certainty of my own survival to consider all that I have lost, what's left to fear?

The first Angel Woolsack said he saw the end of the world, and it may be that he did in his God-wracked mind. But we, sister, have seen it with our eyes, felt it or reared back from it in horror. What have the times taken from you? In our father and his father's time, they lost the honesty of slavery, lost brief violent countries.

Our grandfather wrote like an American prophet. All soaring hope and demented glory. I've tried, but just don't have it in me. Everything sounds weighty if you write it like the Bible.

Now our father's gone to join him, and I've heard by the same channels that your man's been taken from you. Well, so has mine. But like our father mine is never coming back.

All love is risk. Without risk love is worthless, the dead, dry bed of a long, uneventful marriage. Maybe I've risked more than some— the risks of discovery, of death—but that's what it takes to be happy.

No, I still haven't put it right. "Risk" makes it seem as though the stakes are equal for all parties. And they aren't.

What I've done, I've done for myself, for greed, for anger some-times, for Gulf Shipping, for our father, who told me once that the first corporations were chartered by God—the Church and its ministries—and ours was no different. Only rarely have I done some-thing because of love.

The year of the revolution, in 1912, I'd left León and my lover to fight for a side that I knew in my heart was going to lose. Knew because I'd fought on the other side, the government side, more times than I can count. This doesn't make anything right except in my own small soul, and really it wasn't even for that, or because I believed in the Liberal Party, but because I wanted to be something I couldn't.

Do you remember the poem I read that night at Christmas? I heard it first in 1906, not long after it was written by the great Rubén Darío in protest of our snatching of Panama from Colombia, sear-ing verses against the country we come from. This was in León, in a house of some landowner's son who hosted gatherings of literary and moneyed types. I listened with them while a young man I didn't know read the poem aloud. His voice, you could almost hear where adolescent cracks had been. He read, scanning the room with his head inclined, dark eyes darting up from the page to fix on one listener and then the next, but when he was done he was looking straight at me. His face was round and razor-burnt at the jawline, his nose boxer-broad. I didn't know his name yet, and then the others were asking what I—the only Yanqui there—thought of the poem. When I was younger I used to go on about how the borders of the United States had fallen over our state, how we were from a Catholic, Latin place too, a place of slavery and defeat. I used to try and make whoever I was talking to down there understand that I felt no more American than they did, which is to say *exactly* as American. Some of men there that night had heard me talk this way before, but I couldn't find it in me then. I felt revealed, naked, and yet irrevocably separate in my wish for belonging. And maybe this is the problem of being American, your birthright is nothing but motion, your nativity goes back only to the point of the great theft, so we are always looking to be something we never can. Maybe that is why we're always reaching, taking, in the hope that the next thing we grasp will be truly ours. I go into these places, I am hungry for these places in the center and south because a part of me hopes to find or maybe to make a country that matches the country I carry inside me.

Conrad says that the true virility of man is expressed in action of the conquering kind. So I am that conqueror, and when the young man was through with the poem I felt that other rush, stronger than belonging, stronger than the desire to be a part of something—the need to take and possesses, whether it's a scrap of land for railroad or a silver mine or a man.

Before I left León in 1912 for the war, I sat beside the man who'd been the boy who read the poem. We were having coffee and reading the papers, news of the Marines' landing, and he found an editorial written by a mutual friend that said "the blond pigs of Pennsylvania" had invaded "our garden of beauty." I rather liked the turn, but he was angry on my behalf, saying, "Well you aren't a pig."

"And I'm not from Pennsylvania," I said. "Thank God."

Our laughter then like New Year's gunfire, brief and loud and aimed at the sky, and I must remember this moment, his jaw tilted back, throat exposed and Adam's apple jolting ribbed there under the skin, a horizon of white teeth flashed only for me.

What do you remember about your man, now that the country has taken him from you? His voice. His hands on you. I'm not asking you to imagine that I feel whatever you're feeling, that loves are the same, any more than people are. I'm asking you to imagine me feeling, alive.

The place where I died was first settled by the Chorotega Indians and lost in a long and bloody war with the invading Nicaros, who worshipped a god who wore the skins of his enemies over his own.

I crawled out of the ruins of the Hotel Ascarate, pulled myself along by broken things, bleeding from everywhere but whole enough to crawl through the smoke and the smashed furniture and into the plaza where the smoke was thick and blowing. I stood, hearing the voice of the Alabaman calling somewhere in the wreck behind. I limped off across the plaza, toward the Church and, I hoped, a way out. Sounds of rifle fire from the east, the beginning of the assault, cracking louder than the ringing in my ears. Seeing the church steps I thought of lying there and sleeping, but that was just loss of blood. I passed the Church and went into an alleyway, where in the thinned smoke and the light of a cart that had caught fire I saw the Alabaman standing there, hands on his knees, panting. Another shell struck in the plaza and I was thrown to the ground. When the chips of stone had stopped falling the Alabaman had me by the arm, pulling me up. He was holding up his hands, shouting, but I couldn't hear what. He was grinning, and then I knew what he wanted, knew what he would say.

I may be saner than some in our family, but I was still going to kill him. And it wouldn't have mattered if I'd heard the man say to hell with everything, that he wanted to get out of this together. I would've done the same thing and the space it took in my mind is less than what's here on the page.

There in the shadow of the Church of Our Lady of the Assumption I fell forward into the man's chest, and he was trying to hold me up, to help, as I reached with my free hand for the pistol at his side and pulled it loose, cocked the hammer back, and drove the barrel up under his chin and fired once and again.

My hearing would be gone for days, returning first in a seashell whoosh as I entered occupied León, but in that moment the silence gave me an awful clarity as I let his body, which couldn't be said to have much of a head, fall to the dirt of the alleyway. I hurried to take the money from my billfold and pocket it, then slipped my billfold with its papers and identification and even poems—the things that told who I was, who I'd been—into the dead man's jacket, the previous contents of which I took and discarded bit by bit along my way.

I have been in my life Angel Joseph Woolsack and I have been the man in the cream-colored suit and I have been Phillip Nolan and Arthur Lee and Lucien Cartier and I have been just a nod to a boy paid to watch the gate of a house rented under one of these names and I have been a son and a brother and a lover and I have been the killer of others who were themselves sons and brothers and lovers, and I have been the one who wears his enemy's skin. It wasn't that night that I abandoned the name of Angel Woolsack (I'd done that long before), or even on the night with Red and mother and father and you, but this was another, further flight from what that name had meant, and all that was left of it, I imagined, would be in thoughts like yours, our father's, our mother's, even Red's, that poor thing, and, I knew, in the voice of the man I was going back to. Whose name I haven't written yet, and who I've lost now too. To the 'flu, two months back.

His name was Eduard.

There, I've said it.

Now I'll say the harder things and maybe then I can sleep.

◆ ◆ ◆

Three

Dusk of a dank September evening Isaac came back from Biloxi later than he should have, nursing a busted hand. He was late because he hadn't been able to ride the bicycle, couldn't put any weight on his right hand to hold the handlebars without pain gloving him to the wrist. So he had walked the eleven miles home pushing the bike through the last of the summer heat, in the ditches the irises boiling. When he appeared at the bend in the lane that led to their house Kemper ran to him and he was holding up that injured hand in a gesture oddly like victory though his aspect told otherwise. His shirt, she saw, was torn at the collar, his right shoulder clouded with blood.

He sat in the kitchen while Kemper chipped at the half-melted block of ice she'd taken out of the box, and he remembered how she'd hacked at the loaf of sugar in the gone house on Deer Island, and he was smiling when she set the bowl of icewater on the table. She took his hand and dipped it in the water and she tried to understand that smile.

—What are you doing? she said.

—Thinking of you.

—Isaac.

She pulled out a chair and sat beside him. She had never known him to be violent, never known him to fight. The smile left his face and he looked tired and ashamed.

—Please don't lie to me, she said.

He stared at his hand and tried to find the words.

In the following days one Oscar Evans, a citizen of Biloxi, composed a letter to what was then called the Bureau of Investigation. By day Evans was a salesman for an insurance company, a firm-handshaker who held court in barbershops and diners throughout the county. Having learned recently of socialism he bore a special hate for all reddish behavior and so spent an increasing portion of his off-hours as an employee of the American Protective League, a patriot organization which then counted some four-hundred-thousand members in the United States. The concerns of Oscar Evans, who loved his country, and those of the League to which he belonged, were chiefly hostile immigrants, disloyalty, weak-minded liberalism, and the agitations of socialists. In light of the war, the federal government allowed the League to operate with a certain degree of extra-legal license, and though these defenders of the homeland were sworn only to report suspicious activity, their zeal often carried them further. When not harassing German-Americans or stopping young men in the street and demanding to see their draft cards, the members of the League turned their attention to their neighbors, their communities, where dissent and socialism and unmanly refusal to join those who were taking bullets in defense of *your* freedom meant that you deserved, they were fond of saying, a bullet yourself. So they would be vigilant listeners and takers of notes, dispatching their reports to the offices of the bureau, and that was what well-liked and firm-handed Oscar Evans did.

In re: Isaac Patterson (no m.i.)

Disloyal Criticism of Oklahoma Arrests of Aug. 1917

At Biloxi, Mississippi

Employee was notified by Postmaster Gwynn that Tom Wilkins and H. R. Ladner reported that subject was overheard in the workshop of B. Patterson & Co. Stoneworks, Biloxi, Miss., saying that the arrests of slackers and draft rioters in Oklahoma was a "G—d D—d disgrace" and that the war was furthermore illegal, the draft unconstitutional, and other equally inflammatory remarks. Wilkins and Ladner, truck drivers visiting the stoneworks, reportedly then questioned subject's draft status, to which subject replied with unprintable remarks about the draft, Wilkins and Ladner, and J. P. Morgan, at which point Wilkins and Ladner report an altercation occurred leaving the subject with a broken jaw and Wilkins and Ladner respectively with a collapsed eyesocket and split nose (these injuries confirmed by Postmaster Gwynn). The subject is of draft age and unregistered, lives in a settlement between Maurepas and Pascagoula, Miss., and works occasionally as a laborer at B. Patterson's (subj.'s brother) stoneworks. The subject is also a painter of artistic pictures (employee cannot comment on content). Employee proceeded to interview Wilkins and Ladner, as well as B. Patterson, who refused. Employee then attempted to interview subject's parents, also citizens of Harrison County. Subject is adoptive son. After being invited in by Ida Patterson, employee proceeded with preliminary questioning, which was interrupted by Joel Patterson, who ordered employee to leave premises. When employee explained credentials, Espionage Act, etc., Joel Patterson left and reappeared a short time later with a shotgun. Employee left premises unmolested and will continue investigation of Patterson and others, as mentioned in employee's last concerning possible demonstrations and rallies, until otherwise notified or given updated orders.

Yours,

Oscar V. Evans, Cmdr. A.P.L., Ch. 17.8

So Oscar Evans and others like him, who loved their country and those who are said to guard us while we sleep, sent their letters and went about their business, sat at tables while their wives brought supper, cast the same smooth looks of paternal approval on wives and children, if these were scrubbed and appropriately dressed, and slapped them with hands or belts or razor strops if they were not, and despite the fact that others were blind to the present crisis, these men felt, in the quiet accord of dinnertable or desk or favorite chair or churchpew, the awesomeness of their responsibility settle on their heads like a crown, and if you looked close you could see the welcome pain of it in their faces, like a man feels at the end of a good day's work.

A week later Isaac fled bleeding from a meeting of dissenters held in rural Jackson County, one of the few to escape. There had been no such gathering of white and black men in living memory, and even the old men present would not mention the last such instance, known through grandfathers and uncles, an event that had occurred when a group of freedmen and some whites aimed to vote in the election of 1868 and were likewise ridden down and terrorized into a submission maintained by resentment and fear that held for a century and on.

But that night men were together who lived near one another and worked alongside one another, smoking, nodding to music, calling back at the speakers, who read from the *Jeffersonian*, a protest paper run out of Georgia by a man called Tom Watson. From the audience men called out and demanded sheets, and the paper was pieced out and torn to scraps until each man had some shred of it and was a criminal. And others took the stage and described misdeeds across the South, the raids, the arrests, the lamentable accident that befell the guardsmen and federal officers when the bridge they were attempting to cross collapsed into the Chattahoochee River. Cheers then and a blonde-bearded tenant farmer took the stage and sang "Can't Cut the Mustard" to chide an old man at the front who'd lately taken a young wife. The old man climbed onstage and hollered out that he might couldn't cut the mustard but he could still lick the jar. The laughter caught in their throats with the sound of engines nearing and the sweep of headlights through the trees. The trucks and cars coming to brake and men dismounting in the dust and the sodium glow with rifles and axehandles. Running then, screaming, gunshots, a riflebutt across Isaac's forehead. His vision all blood as he veered for the opposite belt of trees, away from the lights and the screaming.

—I told you, she said. I *told* you.

—I know.

—We'll leave, she said. We'll go to Cuba. Mexico . . .

—No, he said. I'll go.

She fought down a surge of violence at his words, the hollow gesture of them. She was thinking of her brother and what it meant to be alone. She wrung his wrist.

—You'll have to outrun me too, she said.

When they stopped at Isaac's parents' house, for a long time no one said a word. What followed was as stark as life itself: they embraced him, his parents, and then they let him go.

Hours later they were at the terminal of the United Fruit Company, waiting on a bench beneath whirring fans to board the steamer from New Orleans to Tampico, Kemper resting her head on his shoulder, asleep. She'd been that way for a little while when Isaac saw the soldiers and the men in suits, notebooks flapping in their hands, come in.

He sat up, tilting the brim of his hat over his bandaged forehead, trying to look like what he for all appearances was: a young husband setting off with his wife on a trip. New suit, tired eyes, nerves betrayed around the mouth. He watched the men come streaming through the doors of the terminal and others springing up from behind newspapers and luggage carts, working their way down the rows of benches asking passengers who appeared of draft age for their registration cards. The soldiers stood beside the doors, men hurrying up now and then to shake their hands, thank them for their service. Isaac leaned to get a better look, but there was the weight of Kemper's head, the warmth of her, and he didn't want to wake her. The smell of her hair. He couldn't see her face, and all the better, for he could imagine it peaceful and not ringed beneath the eyes with black and still-smudged makeup from her tears at the sight of his parents. Now, he saw, a pair of young men a few rows ahead being questioned, the idiot litany of names, ages, places of birth. He tried then, as he would not long after when he stood in a line of naked men and boys awaiting inspection, to assume some of the dignity and remove he'd seen in figure models as a student. He tilted his chin and let his eyes go vacant. He hoped he looked wealthy. He felt an awful awareness of detail: Kemper's cheek warm on his shoulder. Her hat in his lap.

When they came for him Isaac spoke in a whisper and didn't move, as if somehow by sheer gentleness he could keep her from seeing him be taken away. But more than her seeing, he hated the thought of her waking alone.

When the A.P.L. man spoke, asking for his card, Kemper's nails were in Isaac's wrist. He couldn't see her but he knew how her face must look, and she held him as tight as she ever had and then the man wasn't asking anything anymore.

Before he was hauled away Kemper pressed into his shoulder the way she did when they were on the porch, looking up at the painted sky. Where she would lie when she returned home in the days following his arrest and many times thereafter, staring at that sky of ghosts, a letter written in a holding cell or an army barracks limp on the boards beside her. She would be there through the years of his imprisonment, under the unchanging blue whose only clouds were nests of dirt daubers and spiders, and she would be there in 1919 when the man appeared who introduced himself as Rule Chandler and said he'd come to kill her.

PART 5

Rule

1918 – 1919

One

They'd been waiting for him. Two white men in summer suits, parked outside the house where Rule Chandler rented a room, waiting for him to return from his shift at the Perdido Street warehouse of Gulf Shipping. When he came close, the nearest one, a whippy dark-haired man, either Indian or Cajun, showed Rule the pistol on his hip. Rule stopped, gathering himself, as the other man pared off from the car and circled behind him. Mid-November, the air had lost its density and the men coming for him seemed to float. Rule had just enough time to make a fist before they were upon him. Much as he'd considered that his life would likely end at the hands of a white man with a gun, Rule Chandler couldn't help but be somewhat shook.

Once they had him in their car, Rule pressed between them on the front seat as they tore out to the western limits of the city and beyond, the man on the passenger side took out a rice sack and tossed it in Rule's lap, saying to put it on.

When Rule didn't move, the passenger leaned in, saying,

—Come on, *més negre*, don't be dat way.

Before Rule could rear back, the passenger had him by the wrist and the driver was holding the pistol to his head.

—The sack means you won't see, the driver said. And if we're worried about you seeing it means we're worried about you remembering, which means we're operating under the assumption that you'll have brains in your head to remember things by when this is through and not all blown out on the side of the road, yeah?

Rule, breathing hard for the arrested effort, for what it took not to fight, let his arms go slack and, cursing, pulled the rice sack over his own head. Inside the sack smelled of brittle grass and riceflour, and a few grains and hulls stuck to the sweat of his forehead.

Summer of 1918 he'd been twenty-six years old and lived alone, reading dime pulps to the men he oversaw at the warehouse and, in his time alone, devouring the *Tribune* and the *Crisis* when he could get it, even as Du Bois went mad for the war in Europe. In June of that year he'd received his draft deferment as an essential laborer and befriended a white man for the first and only time in his life.

Looking back Rule couldn't say when exactly it had happened, on which night or early morning, on which walk from the warehouse to some bar, but Kerry Egan had appeared, hailed him, and joined him in his step. He did remember what the man first said to him: You're the reader. Rule didn't recognize him at first—faces having a habit of running together in the fog of work, the sweet reek of ripe fruit pouring out of the ships—and it was only when Egan said he worked the sorting line and named his foreman that Rule relaxed a bit. And a bit more when the man began to talk, walking easy beside him, not about ballgames or fights or actresses but books. Writers. Maybe because of his surprise at this, maybe because he was tired from ten hours of labor, head ringing from the groan of winches and pulleys, the clap of crates, the anxiousness that came from seeing to it that none of his crew were knocked unconscious by a gantry arm or had their own arms torn off or flattened like the thumbed end of a tube of cream (as he'd witnessed once), Rule's guard slipped such that he didn't go to the bar he'd originally set out for (where this white man and his running mouth would be an invasion of their respite), heading instead to a place that looked the other way and served both races. He found that he liked this man's company. Liked the quick incisiveness of Egan's talk, which was by turns expansive and unguarded and ran through the night as it would for many after. Those times, after work, they would meet at this or that bar and drink cold beers or California grapewine muddled with leaves of coca, which screwed their jaws tight and honed their speech into darts.

They talked politics and of the war in Europe; they talked of New Orleans, to which Egan had recently come on the heels, he said, of a socialist workers' strike in San Francisco. (The latter fact alone endeared Egan to Rule, who still felt the sting of not being native, though he'd been in the city for most of his life.) They got high and drunk enough that Egan could say aloud in a crowded place that he was a Socialist Internationalist and Rule could call himself a Pan-Africanist who held true with some of the socialist writers (though the race-hatred of Egan's beloved Jack London made the latter impossible for Rule to esteem), and when other men around them overheard these ropy titles and demanded to know what the hell they meant, they were drunk and high enough to fight. But most often they talked of books, the vectors of virulent ideas. Egan had even read some negro writers. (And looking back Rule would be more ashamed of his excitement at this fact than anything.) Rule had to catch himself at times, such was the strangeness of their friendship. Just giving it that name was a dangerous act. It was one thing to work alongside a white man, one thing to fish at the same river or yell at the same boxers—these were acts of anonymity, carried out from the safety of crowds. It was quite another to talk with a white man like this.

But now he realized he'd been basking in Egan's notice; how he'd glossed over certain fool arguments, as we do with friends, that otherwise would've aggravated him; how Egan tried one night, as Irishmen have a habit of doing, to claim that his people had been colonized too. Going on about the Celts' poor treatment at the hands of the British and, later, Americans, as though the best way of meeting minds with a black man was to establish just how much your people (or some vague notion of them) had been treated like niggers by the white world. Which was to assume, he'd said to Egan when pushed to his limit, that nigger is some Newtonian constant by which every swinging dick with a grievance can measure his plight now and forever. Egan had backed off, tried to turn the conversation around, and Rule tried to forget it. One night he asked Egan what the hell an educated man like him was doing slinging fruit in New Orleans, and Egan said, I could ask you the same thing. At the time Rule had liked that. It made him feel good. Egan had drawn him in so close that by the time he told Rule that he was a newspaper writer, working on a story about the illegal shipping of weapons to the government of Mexico, Rule was so wrapped up in him that he told Egan almost everything he knew. Which wasn't a great deal, but he'd seen enough in his shifts to know what Gulf was sending on its boats to Tampico. Shared information that seemed small enough at first, and Egan was smart enough to not press him often. So they went on trading books and pamphlets and spun great webs of ideas in smoky barrooms, at dawn roaring out into the combustible air. And in the heat, the danger of it, Rule's reservations fled. This was a man who believed in good causes; and more, Rule thought, this was a man who could handle himself. But then he couldn't; he'd talked too much, asked too many questions. Said the wrong thing to the wrong person. And now he was in the kind of trouble you don't come back from.

When they'd arrived at the appointed place and the sack had been taken off and he'd gone inside and seen what they had there gagged and bound to a kitchen chair, after some unbearable moments of watching, Rule went down the broken steps of the house and out into the yard. The shut door barely muffling the sounds of what went on inside. He stumbled through the dirt unmarked by any feet save his and those of the men who'd brought him, to the deep shadow beneath an oak, where he tried, like someone at the rotten, spinning tail of a drunk, to make himself vomit.

The property had been a part of a sugar plantation for much of the past two centuries, but the house, once an overseer's, and the land it sat on had seen no tenants, no cultivation, for a long time. The house teetered on its pilings, inner walls colonized by mildew and mold and larger organisms, but whole enough for the purpose at hand. In the coming years the house would serve as incubator to a young man, child of Sicilian immigrants, who gathered indigent orphans there to pool their takes after sessions of pickpocketing in the city, and who, when he was an older and more powerful man noted for both his foul mouth and benevolence to Catholic charities, would be deported to the jungles of Guatemala in the efforts of our nation's first Catholic president to yoke organized crime even as he employed, according to his successor, a *goddamn Murder Incorporated* in Latin America, out of whose mountains the Sicilian would emerge in time to play a part in ending the young Catholic president's life.

Everywhere you look is imprinted with its own history of iniquity (and will play host to worse), and so Rule Chandler, when he could urge nothing more from his stomach, went out from the tree down a run lined with shacks that had once housed men and women, lives bought and sold. Not far beyond, the fields that had owned their days. Though Rule had lived in New Orleans from the time he was a boy, his family had come from a rural parish to the southwest. His mother and father, his sisters, had returned there years back, believing life better out in the reeds and he'd found his absolution in the pavement and stone and endless streets, the purity of electric light. But even still he was awake to the land, to the smell on the air from some distant farm, fields smoking, sugar cooking. He'd turned from that life, and Rule supposed he could turn now and run. Between the cabins like the gaps in teeth, the fields, and, farther on, the marsh stood overgrown and waiting. Tell yourself you're somewhere else, he thought. No doubt that's what the man bound to the chair was doing, or had done while he could. What we all do in moments of abandonment and pain. Tell yourself that these sounds are something else and the sight you fled from isn't real and the broken thing in there is not your friend and those are not his muffled screams. That what happened to him isn't your business anymore and now all you have is your own life to save. Tell yourself he lied to you, he put you here casually as you might give directions to a stranger. Anger now, doubled by the knowledge that as bad as what had happened was, what was coming would be worse.

When Rule returned to the house, Woolsack was waiting for him on the steps.

There were five of them there. The driver, the other man, Rule, Egan, and this Woolsack. At first, when Rule heard one of the men address the young man with blood-red hair as Mr. Woolsack, Rule didn't believe them. The Woolsack he'd seen before was a stooped old man, hard-bitten in a way few rich men are. Son, it was rumored, of a slaver, a gentleman of storied violence. This Woolsack was his age or just a little older, thick muscled, though of the kind gotten from iron weights and physical culture rather than work.

Seeing Rule approach, Red Woolsack wiped his brow, fingers lingering on his face like a bald man checking a toupee. Smiling, Woolsack said it was time they had a chat. And that smile was like nothing Rule had ever seen, sort of patched on.

—Feeling better? Woolsack said.

—Not particularly, Rule said. Nobody wants to see a thing like that.

—No, but then you'd be surprised at what some people want.

Rule took out a pack of All-Star cigarettes and lit one.

—Be frank, he said. Ain't much would surprise me anymore.

—Don't ain't me, Woolsack said, voice suddenly harsh. Don't pretend to be stupid. It's insulting, and worse it's a lie.

Rule winced. There were tricks to living, to avoiding death or gaining favor or trust, and playing dumb was one. Let your language slip low as your gaze should go, as though whatever white being stood before you was as magnificent and confounding as a pyramid in the sun.

—It's an awful thing, being lied to. Woolsack turned to Rule. Isn't it.

—It is.

—If you counted all the lies you'd been told your whole life, you'd go crazy.

—You might that.

—You would. He was speaking slowly now, to the dark beyond them. You know that Egan in there lied to you. Put you in this with his lies. But it never starts with lies outright, does it. He told you what he really did . . . what he was planning to do to me and my business.

—He told me he was studying working conditions. Said he was a journalist, working—

Woolsack went *tsk*, as if something had hurt him.

—Don't call it that, Woolsack said.

—What?

—Don't call what they do journalism.

—What would you call it?

—Lying. In person or on paper, it doesn't matter. It's still telling people lies. Putting words in their mouths and voices in their heads so that they . . .

Woolsack made a fist as if to catch the loose end of his sentence and then went quiet.

—So what am I here for?

—You see, Woolsack said. Egan there took you for exactly what you pretended to be just now, when you tried to nig' it up. Just a dumb ole *good one*. But you aren't like that. I can see it.

Rule turned his head at the sound, coming from inside, of something heavy being dragged across the floor.

—I want you to think, right now, Woolsack said. Did you tell him anything you wish you hadn't?

Rule could think of many things. But they were not about this man's business or workers' strikes or the guns that Gulf Shipping was illegally sending to Mexico. They were about his own life, what he had known. He cursed himself for these and all the ways he had betrayed everything that his life and the lives of others had taught him.

Woolsack stood and waved for him to do the same.

—When we go inside, he said, I'm going to offer you a choice.

Woolsack shut the door behind them and Rule stood before the body bound to the chair in the center of the room. Egan's wrists were tied to the chairlegs, fingers bent at strange angles. At his feet lay a hurricane lamp, bell-glass flecked with blood so that the light thrown on the rotting walls was patterned with spots of darkness. Rule spoke the bound man's name, but the head hung limp, the twisted hands lay still. Face swollen out of all proportion, arms like those of a whorehouse sofa, torn, discolored, spotted with the black divots of cigarette burns; only the pop of blood in bubbles from one nostril to tell that the man was still breathing. Beyond him some movement in the dark, and from the far corner the driver approached, stripped to the waist and sweating, ready to resume his work, but Woolsack told him to wait.

From the pocket of his coat Woolsack produced a pistol. A Smith & Wesson Model 1899. He flipped the gun in his hand and held it out grip-first, to Rule.

—Take it.

Rule made no move. The driver and the other man were muttering.

—Go on, Woolsack said.

The men in the dark came forward now, uneasy glances to their boss and at Rule.

—Easy now, Woolsack said to them. And when Woolsack offered the pistol for the third time, Rule took it.

The great weight of metal, his palm slick on the grip. He couldn't look at it.

—It's not right, said the second man. A neg' to shoot a white man.

—No, Woolsack said, locking eyes with Rule. It'll be him.

The second man began to speak, but the driver beside him held up a hand in warning.

—You see, Rule, Woolsack said. Mr. Cormier here thinks just the same of you as this man, Egan, did.

Woolsack stepped closer and reached out, embracing the pistol and the hand that held it, as if to impart some strength. His eyes trembling on the verge of something.

—He thinks you're a nigger, Woolsack said. But I know different.

Woolsack stared, seeing in Rule's expression an affirmation of this knowledge. What Woolsack had sensed the moment he'd first seen him. There was a blessed silence around Rule Chandler, a silence Woolsack could find in the presence of an increasingly precious few. Only those he could trust. With others, like these two here, his head filled with voices. The voices he'd heard first around the age of eighteen, whispers in the dark, and which came in chorus shortly after Red Woolsack's twenty-second birthday, when he was newly married. At first he could make no sense of what they said, but as time wore on and the voices took purchase he found they spoke small, troubling truths. Warnings. When he first heard the voices he thought his house was haunted; then they followed him to work; they spoke when he was alone and he thought himself possessed; then they spoke in the presence of others and he searched the faces of those around him, pleading silently for them to say they could hear the voices too. But he could ask nothing outright for fear of being thought mad, and so he was alone in his suffering and there were times he wept, so great was his loneliness and so dire the warnings he heard. Until the time came when he understood what he was being told, of the dangers everywhere and the system arrayed against him, all-encompassing and complex. It was as though he'd been gifted with a new kind of perception, a keyhole into the minds of all those who wished him harm. He began to listen and to feel, for the first time in his life, that he was not alone.

All this behind Woolsack's eyes. What Rule knew was that he would not leave this place alive unless he did as this man said, and likely not even then. He felt drugged. It was as if a great hole had torn open in the floor before him and the pistol was an anchor dragging him toward the edge where he would fall forever. And on the other side was Egan, who had begun to move. Who raised his head.

—He brought you into this, Woolsack said. Now you get yourself out.

It does not make Rule Chandler a better man that he wondered in those madness-choked moments whether he could shoot the two men and Woolsack before they could kill him. The driver and his partner had their hands at their hips, waiting for a word from Woolsack, who looked on with eyes bizarrely pleading. As if Rule were the crazy one to refuse his offer.

—All right Rule, he said. Let's get it over with.

There was no space for sanity in that room. Rule raised the pistol level with Egan's ruined face, the swollen forehead nodding to him, almost offering.

Rule squared his body and hoped that his hand wouldn't shake as he aimed the sight between the things that had once been eyes but were now beaten so that it was incredible to imagine that they had ever seen the sky or a lover or a mother or, as they did now, a crack opening in the weltered flesh, a friend.

Rule remembered seeing, when he was maybe eight, a group of men on the corner of Fourth Street one summer evening reading from a paper in voices not loud or broken but horribly flat, of the lynching of a black man in the city of Atlanta. Pieces of the lynched man's body had made their way into the reliquary of whiteness. His heart sent to the governor of Georgia, his right hand kept in the display window of a downtown Atlanta grocer, where it was seen by W. E. B. Du Bois on his way to a meeting with the white man who invented Remus. The men in the crowd cussing, mumbling, locked there together on the corner taxed once more with the knowledge of this possible fate. The boys at the curb seeing now the anger and the fear in the faces of the men they admired. Rule among them, watching. Listening to what it meant to live and to die. There are men who shoot and men who get shot, they said. You might get shot anyway, even if you're strong and carrying. But at least you had a chance. You might take one with you, which meant you might at least have satisfaction in death. You might be dead before they got you, which meant they would put your eyes out and hack off your hands and your balls and light you on fire and laugh while you burned.

The men on the streetcorner a chorus of negation.

I won't, they were saying. I won't go down that way. They'll have to kill me first.

Rule notched the hammer. The trigger went back and back and seemed like it would never fire.

It does not make him a worse man that he wanted to live.

Two

He was given the pistol and further instruction on its use. He was given money and the promise of more to come when, as Woolsack said, there was more such work to do. In the coming days Rule kept to his room, on the top floor of a camelback house owned by a woman from Haiti who lived on the ground floor with her husband, a jeweler, and two children, girls, and asked no questions of the tenants.

He settled into a kind of nightmare softness. Given nothing to do for weeks, he drank more than usual, to steady his mind, and ate the food brought by the Haitian woman's daughter, a long and faintly freckled thing named Augustine, who was much too old to be going into men's rooms but didn't so much as glance at him anyway, leaving the dish on the sideboard and slipping out; so he sat alone and put on fat for the first time in his life. He couldn't sleep and couldn't bring his mind to read, and so lay for hours in bed with catalogs propped open, taking pulls from a bottle of rye and imagining which presents he'd send home. Imagined his parents, his cousins, slack-jawed before a pile of crates.

That winter he took part in the burning of a pair of warehouses, the bludgeoning of their guards. He found that, drunk, he didn't mind the work.

In February he learned that dynamite weeps.

In March, at carnival, he rolled the accountant of a fruit wholesaler. In April he ransacked offices and went with the driver to slip a bomb in the wheel well of a car. But at that time he'd only killed one man.

He drank down what visions arose to trouble him in the night. He got himself measured for a new suit. He went to the red-light district, streets full of soldiers chasing their hard-ons, and gave himself over to whoring. A stint that ended when he could no longer take the braying stupidity of everyone around him, the money-flinging fools who fought to be the loudest and the dumbest in the room. So he went back home, and whenever one of Woolsack's men came calling, he did what was asked of him, and well; and in between he ate and drank and it took more and more to make him feel anything at all, as though something in him had been dulled. A callus grown over the man he'd been.

And when he saw himself in shop windows or in the great, gleaming walls of barbershops, he was amazed not at the change but the lack of it. He expected to see someone else.

He wondered what his boyhood self would think of the man he'd suddenly become. When he was seven years old Rule's family left the country around Terrebonne in the receding southern tip of the state for the city of New Orleans, where his father went to work at a slaughterhouse and his mother as a cleaner. To the child Rule the city was a wild wonder, and he couldn't understand why his parents went about always with their eyes averted from the buildings and machines. They lived with his aunts and an uncle, a swarm of cousins, in a tenement building on

Saratoga Street, and six days a week Rule went to work as a hand at a lumberyard near the river in cleated boots too big for his feet. Heading to or from work and in the hours between he ran with the aforementioned cousins and other children, drawn always to the doings of the neighborhood men. Not those late of the countryside like their own fathers, but city men. Objects of awe (if they carried themselves well) or derision or shame (if they did not), but always fascination. Men in suits and bowler hats, watchchains at their hips, and women who wore bright, tight dresses, women whose hair was ironed and whose arms were rolled with fat. Men who did not squabble but were good with a joke and might, winking, tell a dirty one in passing to the boys who lingered at the periphery of their conversations. And maybe because Rule was a more dutiful son than most and would do little that might disappoint the father who'd used most of his strength to get them out of the countryside and to the city and the rest on the killfloor of Union Slaughterhouse, he was drawn less and less to the men who gambled and joked and dazzled but to one who possessed few of their seeming virtues and fewer still of their vices. Here was a man who held no streetcorner court, who gambled and drank socially, who kept his assignations with women private and yet wore the sharpest suits, got of a Poydras Street Jew who would later testify to his character when that man became notorious. Here was a man who read: generally works on politics and the literature of the Pan-Africanist movement and in particular the International Mission Society, which had formed a cooperative movement to buy its members tickets to a new life in Africa, and whose pamphlets he distributed each month. Later it would be discovered that the Society was backed by a white Alabaman Klansman, but by the time of his death, the man, whose name was Robert Charles, had paid some $200 toward his own exodus.

A neighborhood eccentric, Robert Charles, appearing at your door with his bundle of the *Voice of Missions*, whose learning and earnestness might have made him an object of sport were it not for the fact that he was known (as neighbors would later attest) as a man not to be trifled with. He did contract work, scouting labor, and he stayed in a little room in an alley off Fourth Street, between Rampart and the tenement where Rule and his family lived. Close enough that Rule could stop by on his way home from work and, if Robert Charles was home and willing, sit with the man and listen to him read, then as time went on be made to read himself. Robert Charles's manicured finger moving patiently under the words. A gentleness that never failed to stun Rule after a day of being hollered at and the *whup* of falling lumber; Robert Charles's measured voice filling the room. But there was that other side to Robert Charles, no less fascinating, the side that loved firearms.

He'd left Copiah County, Mississippi, knowing how to hunt, but there was another way of handling a gun, which Robert Charles learned at the age of twenty-one when he went to join his brother Hank in Vicksburg, where he worked digging holes and laying pipe for the coming miracle of running water (which would never reach his parents' home). Their shovels turned up trenches and fortifications, unexploded shells and black boles of cannon and human bones cut to their marrow. The place was filled with feral dogs that skulked as offal thieves and child-maulers, and men who were not much better. Everyone was armed, and soon Robert Charles was no exception.

When the digging was done Robert Charles was the owner of a side-ejecting Samuel Colt's in .44 caliber and he chose to remain in the grave-ringed town, taking work as a section hand on the L.N.O.&T. railroad. With his paycheck he was able to make rent, buy his meals and drinks, and even, now and then, newspapers, books, pen and ink and paper—purchases that felt more illicit than the guns, which he also continued to acquire.

He had to. After two years in Vicksburg he knew more men who'd been shot than hadn't. Men he worked alongside or drank with at the saloons on Levee Street, where each night at midnight the music and the laughter and the singing had to cease for one hour by order of the law so that white passengers on red-eye trains would not be disturbed by black voices, black existence. The people in the barrooms would fall silent, women's laughter dried up, and men who were loud as thunder would go stony.

He could still see them, he told Rule. Men who had been or would be shot by cousins or by wives; by storekeepers out of suspicion and by themselves out of despair; by strangers as was one man called Dick Deadeye when a white stoker from a stopped train caught Dick watching him piss out behind the watertower early one morning (shooting Dick through the eye and giving him his nickname); and more than a few by Constable John Stanley of the Vicksburg police. One of those peacekeepers who, we must remember, have more to fear from us—potential havocs that we are with our mysterious and ever-shifting hands, bodies crackling with the potential to impede the lawman's much desired return home—than we from them with their weapons and legal infallibility. On Levee Street and the surrounding neighborhoods John Stanley was known mostly as a man who rarely resorted to words when the means of violence were at hand, and, if you asked certain people, for keeping a black mistress. A rumor bloodily confirmed one August night when this mistress shot John Stanley through the side during an argument, at which point John Stanley put a bullet in her head and four more into her brother, who'd heard the first shot and come from next door. Add to these an L.N.O.&T. porter who had the misfortune of being on the street when John Stanley came roaring out. In the coming days and to the shock of many Constable John Stanley was indicted by a grand jury. The jurors, it must be said, were more concerned with Stanley's miscegenation than the murder of two unarmed black men and one armed black woman, but still the people of Levee Street hoped for, and more importantly collected money to bribe the presiding judge into rendering, a conviction.

But when the hat was passed Robert Charles didn't give a dime. He saved his money, and when John Stanley was found not guilty and set free, Robert Charles owned another gun.

Why put your money toward a justice that won't come, he'd said to Rule, when you can have justice, or at least the hope of it, there with you. In your hand.

Rule remembered him among the men on the streetcorner, saying Never. And now he wondered what Robert Charles, who before his own death in July of 1900 would become infamous, would've thought of the man Rule had become.

Rule hurrying in from the summer rain. Three months before the influenza would come south, four months from the end of the war. He kicked off his boots and sat at the end of his bed and cast about for whiskey. On the floor, just past the lip of the door, lay a postcard.

That night he'd broken the leg of a ship's mate while the driver held a gun to the head of its captain. A foolish man who'd balked when he found out about the guns being laid in the hold of his ship. Given his first and only warning.

—Now's not the time to be a patriot, the driver said.

The mate on the floor of the wheelhouse, screaming.

Rule in his room, later, holding the postcard. It had come from home, written by his cousin but in the voice of his whole family, thanking him for the things he'd sent. Telling him to visit. For a while he thought of the cane fields and sunlight on the water in the rice paddies. Then he was thinking of the oldest daughter of the Haitians, and that maybe she'd been the one to slip this mail under his door. That she'd thought of him.

A week later he robbed two consuls of a Central American nation as they exited a whorehouse. Took their valises, which he brought to the man who would bring them to Woolsack, and their billfolds, which he gave to a child he saw who seemed particularly ragged. The child was white, as had been the men he'd robbed, and bore no gratitude in his face. Rule walked on, and the next morning read in the *Picayune* about what he'd done, only in the article he was some random negro, a part of the mass of faceless criminals distinguished only by skincolor. In this way he was able to, at a moment's notice, slip from full view into a maligned undercurrent of blackness. Helpful as this was in certain situations, it spelled a larger doom. It made life horrifically random. You were all equally suspicious, and so equally dangerous and thus deserving of whatever came.

What came to Robert Charles, in late July of 1900, when he was thirty-five and Rule was still a little boy who'd only catch terrifying glimpses of the events of that day, hidden by his father in the windowless interior of their apartment while the gunfire and the crowds raged outside, was infamy. It began as these things do, with a pair of young black men, waiting. Robert Charles and a friend waiting for their dates, who hadn't shown by midnight. Waiting at the corner of two mythologies, the intersection of Dryades and Washington streets; one named for the goddesses of trees, admonishers of senseless destruction of woodland, and the other for the American god whose divinity was first glimpsed when he forthrightly admitted to cutting one down. Like many in New Orleans at that time, the neighborhood where they waited was mixed, blacks living alongside whites with circumspection if not amity, and one of these neighbors, seeing from his window two strange negroes waiting on the steps of a house down the block, told his wife to lock the door behind him and went out looking for a patrolman, found two.

The space of a minute in a policeman's presence is a maddeningly condensed trial; you are arraigned by all American history on charges of being born. And in that span, when one patrolman drew his pistol and the other his club, Robert Charles rose. A gun in his hand. Before the next minute was out, Robert Charles had blown the knee off one patrolman and sent the other running, which he himself did, leaving his bewildered friend behind.

The police found Robert Charles at his room off Fourth Street, or rather he found them, stepped out into the alley shoulder slung with bags containing spare rounds and a little instrument he'd ordered through an ad in *Scientific American,* a tool that reloaded shells spent by the Winchester repeating rifle he held now at his shoulder, the rifle he aimed then and fired, killing the precinct captain who'd come to claim him. Killed two more in the street as he fought his way to a tenement building, where he barricaded himself in an upper room and rained hell for two days on the riotous white crowd that massed below. Body after body in the buckhorn sight of his rifle. He picked them off carefully, one round a minute, as crowds of outraged citizens grew, thousands spilling from the foot of the statue of Robert E. Lee at what was once Tivoli Circle, which they circled like pilgrims at Kaaba.

Robert Charles kept firing, and Rule Chandler, not yet ten, heard it all. Heard the police break down the doors of the adjacent building, smelled the smoke of the fire they set. Then all was confusion and the corpse of Robert Charles was hauled into the street where, amid the usual mutilations, the child of a dead patrolman was brought forth to stamp on Robert Charles's face.

When the killing was done, in the city of New Orleans and throughout the country, people sent up great peals of support for the police and tried to place the blame for Robert Charles. They blamed the man who sold him the gun; they blamed the Devil; they blamed black nationalists; they blamed the black family as an institution; they blamed newspapers for their coverage of lynchings; they blamed drugs and drink; they blamed his nature. Some even claimed he was incensed over the killing of some negro in Atlanta.

It was, Rule thought, like blaming a flashflood on a random raindrop.

◆ ◆ ◆

October 1918. More Americans would die that month than in any other, before or since. The influenza swift as the bolts of their doors, which must be shut on order of the city council.

At this time, and against his better judgement and the darkening course of his life, Rule Chandler fell deeply in love with Augustine, the oldest daughter of his landlord. It started back when he held the postcard and went on through the following months as he made more frequent appearances at the dinnertable, listening to her, trying to watch her without being noticed, as did the other unmarried boarders and not a few of the married ones. When she was not helping her mother in the house, Augustine worked part time at the counter of a store down the street, until the stores closed for the 'flu. Like her mother, she moved with the sense that everything she did was somehow beneath her, and for months looked at Rule as if he notched well lower than herself.

Until she didn't. And it might have been the quarantine or the threat of imminent death (which does strange things to hearts), but whatever the reason one night in November, just before the signing of the armistice, she appeared in his bedroom doorway, asking to be let in.

Her family, so the story went, had once been great. Her father, a small pensive man, light-skinned and spectacled, a jeweler now by trade, had been an official in the Haitian government during the seven years of seven presidents. Days before he was taken away by the officers of the fourth president, he'd used what remained of his wealth to ship his wife and daughter out of the country. Then this small, gentle man was sent to the island of Gonâve, where he spent almost a year heading out each day at dawn shackled by the ankle to another prisoner to work in the limestone quarries, until one evening on the march back from their work he and his companion made an escape. A few days later he appeared at a village on the northwest coast of the island and there convinced a fisherman to ferry him across the windward pass to Cuba, but not before having a blacksmith remove from his ankle the shackle which, the story went, was still attached to what remained of his companion, a foot and swollen shin. You would never know by looking at him—this little, balding man with his fine hands—that he was capable of such a thing, but you might catch a glimpse in the eye of his daughter. A glint as sharp as the smirk that swept up the corner of her mouth when she finished telling Rule the story.

—Are you shocked? she said.

She was sitting on the edge of his unmade bed, legs crossed. Still wearing makeup even though she hadn't left the house for weeks.

—Nope.

—Really? she said, her eyes losing themselves somewhere past him.

—Well, maybe a little, he said.

His thumb pressing her hooked mouth.

—But I wouldn't be so shocked if you'd said it had been you.

The glint so sharp and bright now it cut him in two. He wanted to live there forever in that gleam, like in the bow of the moon.

He loved this look and tried to get it out of her as often as he could; those days of being trapped, when he had nowhere to go and nothing in the world but her; he loved her faint freckles and how she said *ris* instead of rice; loved how she talked about where she'd lived with her family outside Port-au-Prince in a neighborhood of mostly German millionaires. She'd been eight years old when she and her mother left, but she kept her country among the glossy recollections the rich have of their childhoods. Her words, for a while at least, keeping his mind from darker places, from what he'd seen and what he went on seeing. What he'd done, and what he'd be asked to do.

Three

Until quite recently Kemper Woolsack had taken for granted the fact that her parents' chests would rise and fall, their lungs fill with air, their hearts go on beating even after she had banished them from her own. Regardless of the distance she put between herself and her parents, she took comfort in this certainty, much in the same way that a person locked away from the sun and the moon must believe that those bodies still exist in their former places, doing what they've always done, because to allow yourself to think otherwise means you've come into another world.

Now at the age of twenty-five Kemper had been there, when Isaac couldn't, for the deaths of his mother and father, she from a cancer of the breast and he a few months later from what could only be called grief, unguarded people whose warmth and kindness she had come to love but also mistrust, never understanding how they could give so much of themselves so freely, and perhaps it was this mistrust Isaac's brother and sister-in-law sensed when they sent her away from their father's memorial service. Their eyes on her as if to say, Go watch your own parents die. Go have your own grief.

And now she would.

Mid-December. A shroud of cold thrown over the city filled with returned troops and men selling bonds for a war that had been over for weeks, death now in the form of the 'flu sweeping through the cities and towns. White masks in the streets. Word of deaths by the thousand elsewhere. One afternoon Rule woke to shouting in the street below and hurried down with the pistol in his belt. The Haitians and some of their boarders were on the sidewalk, necks craned, looking at the sky where little sheets of paper fell in drifts. Then he saw them: airships, silver-bellied and tapered like fish, drifting high above the city. He looked up, jaw slack, all wonder and horror, the polarities of that age. The war was over, he'd gone out with Auga in their masks to celebrate the day, but here they were, still selling it. He snatched a sheet from the air and read its message—that a German bombing would be just like this if you did not BUY WAR BONDS.

When she arrived in town for her father's funeral in January of 1919, it had been over a year since Kemper last set foot in New Orleans. The day of Isaac's arrest, the curtain rising on sixteen months of dissolution and despair that saw her rarely leave the property on the coast, speaking to fewer and fewer people as the pandemic reached into the towns and the houses of her neighbors so that there was no one to speak to even if she'd wished.

In the city many still went about in white paper masks, though the worst was said to be over and across the country quarantines were being lifted. She saw them hurrying by as she made her way from the depot to the streetcar line, old men with their lapels arched, women carrying cakes wrapped for the Epiphany night. Soldiers in their uniforms walking with gallant limps until they were sure no one was looking; hollow-eyed veterans in streetclothes. She tried not to stare but searched their features, their lost faces, imagining how Isaac might be when he came home. She had his letters and the letters from the parole board with her, tucked in the inner pocket of her gray coat like passports to the life she hoped to have again. Now and then as she made her way through the city, she would reach into her coat and finger an edge of the paper. She touched the letters and felt her chest go tight, as it had for days, and at any given moment she couldn't be sure which moved her, hope or grief.

She rode into the Garden District, crossing down from St. Charles and heading toward the river. Past the whitewashed walls of the Lafayette Cemetery, where her father's stone stood ready, as it had for years, in this unfashionable burial ground catty-corner to the stele of the Poydras orphans. She hurried from this place already featured in guidebooks, hating this city that loves the dead more than the living.

The house she'd grown up in was mazed with flowers sent by admirers and associates, current and former heads of state, whose cards of condolence were displayed with appropriate prominence. She didn't recognize the servant who let her in, the woman disappearing by the time Kemper was winding through a tunnel of white-throated lilies to the front room where her father's body was being kept. She'd read stories in the papers of corpses in the no-man's-lands of Belgium glowing in the night as they rotted, and as she came closer to the coffin the body of her father seemed to give off a faint glow. And there beside it sat her mother.

Pale hair veiled in black, small, sunken in a wingbacked chair, Marina sat with her eyes downcast so that Kemper couldn't tell at first whether her mother was awake or if she'd been lulled asleep by the oppressive smell of flowers in the air. Kemper knelt beside her and touched her mother's hand and, aching, watched the woman's shawled shoulders lift, her chest expand and ease, just as Marina had watched in pain and awe the first swell of her only daughter's purple ribcage and had observed this same action for months and years afterwards, just as it was when Marina opened her eyes now and saw her daughter there.

The night of his father's wake, Red Woolsack had Rule Chandler brought to his house. Rule hadn't seen the man in many months but had heard through others in Woolsack's pay about the old man's death.

The man at the door didn't speak, merely let Rule in and shut the door after him. Rule heading down a narrow hallway, the wall pressing his shoulders close as a slaughterhouse chute. The hall opened on a small room, the offshoot of a kitchen, and there sat Woolsack. Dressed in half-buttoned pajamas, his feet bare on the tile, Woolsack was staring at his hands which lay flat on the table. Just beyond them, a pistol and the stock of what looked to be a shotgun half in shadow.

—Did you grow up in New Orleans, Rule?

—I did, he said. But some in Terrebonne Parish, out in Tigerville if you know it.

—Is that near Cut Off?

—Near enough.

—I heard they used to bury people up to their necks out there and wait for the tide to come in.

Rule laughed, but stopped when he saw Woolsack's face change.

—It's not funny, Woolsack said.

—No, boss.

—Well, I grew up here, Woolsack said. And I should've left a long time ago. I think a couple hundred years should be plenty for a family to be any one place. Especially here, where everyone you meet can't stop lying. And why should they? It's a city that can't stop lying. It's *built* on a fucking lie (he stamped his foot) that this ground can hold.

So they have their idiot traditions and bring in idiots to see them and fill guidebooks up with ghosts. Ghosts but not the massacres or the killings that made them. And since ghosts aren't real, we can love them. Put them in the guidebooks.

His hands lay flat on the table and he studied them now. The pistol and the shotgun not far away. And he didn't look back at Rule when he next spoke.

—What is there about a ghost that could frighten anyone but a child, he said.

—I don't know, Rule said.

—I think I do. And it's not the ghost itself, it's that if a ghost exists, then there's a life after this, and if there's a life after this then there must be a god who owns it. Right?

Rule said he understood, though he didn't. Any time he was in this man's presence, he tried his best to let most of what he said just burn up on the air like matchheads.

—My grandfather believed in God, Woolsack said. He started out as a preacher. Not that that makes you a believer, but he was. He wrote his own gospel at the end of his life, and I can't say whether it's more or less truthful than the ones bound up in the Book.

—What kind of preaching did he do?

—I wasn't there, I only read him. He came down here before this was a state, when people notched the ears of thieves. Got into revolutions against the Spanish, then against the Americans after the purchase. Do you know who Aaron Burr is?

—Shot Alexander Hamilton.

—Well my grandfather ran with him. And when Burr failed he decided to go into business and started slaving. He lived a long time doing that, and when he was old he wrote his gospel, sure as hell the world was coming to an end. Woolsack sighed. When I was little and I read his book I'd get scared, about the end.

For the first time since Rule had come into the room, Woolsack lifted his hands from the table. Let his hands clasp gingerly, as if they'd been fighting and he'd kept them separate until now.

—God's the frightening thing, Woolsack said. Not the shadow, but what throws it.

Rule nodded.

—Is there anything, Woolsack asked, that you'd be afraid to do? Woolsack eyed him. Or maybe not afraid, but reluctant.

—You wouldn't want somebody who was.

A clarity came over Woolsack's eyes. No, he said, he wouldn't. And that clarity ran straight through to his mind, burning up the voices like a fog. It was in that clarity, in the days after his father's death, that he'd come to the decision to have his sister killed.

Do not confuse madness with cruelty; like society itself, whose strength lies often in the weakness of its members, the frailty of his mind's grasp had kept him from saying what he'd wanted for a long time now. From the moment Kemper turned away from him on her twenty-first birthday, from the moment she took her shares, what should be his, took his parents' love, what should be his. Siblings have, in the wake of a moneyed death, destroyed each other for less. And when he asked Rule Chandler to kill her when she returned to her place in Mississippi in the days after the funeral, Red Woolsack was utterly sane.

Kemper kept the vigil with her mother and they spoke that night as they hadn't in years, or ever. Kemper told her about Isaac, about where they lived, the animals and birds, and the island to which she rowed on cool, calm days, at first to escape the house and the ghost of him everywhere, only to find that the islands held even more of him.

—No children yet, her mother said flatly.

—No.

—Not even any dead?

—No.

—Well, it took us a long time too.

Two days earlier Kemper had been on a nameless spit of sand, crouched before a flock of curlews brought short of their migration by a front. She'd seen so many things born and hatched, these beings on their thousand-mile journeys driven by the impulse that lit in them like a coil of electric filament, something she herself did not possess. For a moment she was worried to tell her mother this, and yet she did say it.

Marina raised her thin gloved hands and talked as if she hadn't heard what her daughter said. Started a story about a lady, an American émigré in Havana who'd started a campaign to end the practice of bullfighting on the island, and had tried to enlist Marina to the cause.

—I told her it was a bad American habit to take away things that don't belong to you in the first place. And this woman said to me, But aren't you American, Mrs. Woolsack? No, I said. I'm what we all are on this side of the ocean, what you are too, I said to her, if you'd admit it. And what is that? We're like the mist, I said. We blow in, we settle, then we burn off and are gone.

Kemper looked to her father's casket, lit now with candles.

—Where's Red?

—He's at home with his family. Sick.

—The 'flu?

—No, thank God. He's just exhausted.

—Sorry to hear he's doing poorly.

Her mother turned, glaring for a moment.

—He was the one, her mother said. He was the one who was with your father at the end.

—He could've told me.

—Could he, dear? Her mother glared at her for an instant before letting her eyes ease. Anyway, she said, it was too sudden.

They were quiet for a long time. Dawn came, the windows beaded and ran. Kemper had fallen asleep and awoke to her mother's chair empty, Marina standing over the body of her husband. Hearing Kemper stir, she spoke without turning.

—I wasn't with him either. She said this as a matter of fact, without regret. They had, Marina said, been together for too long. Marked each other. There's no room in all that for regret.

Kemper smiled at her mother and she thought of marks and what we leave behind, seated simultaneously in love and judgement, as children often are. Now she went to her mother, who was lost deep in her thoughts of a time before she was a mother, before she had been given what the years had steadily taken away.

When she was sixteen and it was already too late, Marina had learned the secret of women and men. Not the act of lovemaking, with which she was relatively familiar, and its consequence, childbirth, which she'd witnessed a few times from the far corner of a room, but something deeper and more final. The sort of thing a mother tells her daughter. You will love them, be shaped by them, shape them, be ruined by them. And there is nothing you can do unless you choose to destroy yourself.

Now on the morning of her husband's burial Marina stands between his corpse and her daughter. Kemper looking as if she is waiting for her mother to say something. What does she want to hear? What is there left to say that hasn't already been said in the twenty-five years of this child's life? Marina steps away from the casket as the mourners begin to arrive, coming through the flowers, and she will not speak. She is locked in silence and every moment readying for the greater silence still to come.

Four

Ghosts filing through the graveyard gates, that's what they looked like. But not the ghosts of a single moment in time, as those of a housefire or a trainwreck might be—all bound together by the common circumstance of their deaths—these people seemed like the ghosts of many pasts, moving parallel to one another and all blind.

Rule at his appointed place, at one end of the side-street entrance to the cemetery, watching them. This family. The oldest ghost, the mother, in a black lace shawl walking under her own power, which seemed considerable, followed closely by the daughter. Broad-backed for a woman and darker than the rest of them, she was the only one who looked up from the pathway and saw him. A tired glance at Rule through the mesh of her veil, and for a moment she seemed to recognize him. Rule nodding gravely, the woman going on with that look still wearing her face. She hadn't met him yet, though the day was coming when she would. Last the son, whose shoulders were supported by a pair of suited men Rule didn't recognize but knew by their wagging jowls were not the kind of men he needed fear. No, he caught himself, they're exactly the kind. The son who paid Rule to watch him, to watch the wife and children who lived increasingly in fear of him, to watch his house and his office. And who knew how many other men like Rule there were; there might be one at every corner of the cemetery, to ensure the safety of the man who was now so nearly destroyed Rule thought a stiff wind might carry him away. Red Woolsack had not left his father's side for the three weeks it took the old man to die of pneumonia, at first slipping notes out to servants, then having a telephone line (which the old man couldn't otherwise abide) run into the sickroom. And when he emerged and the old man was dead, Rule heard first then saw for himself, Woolsack was broken. Or broken worse. Whatever there had been of him, that sorry struggle you could see happening behind his eyes was gone.

That night Augustine came to his room. Past midnight, he was lying beside her in bed, watching how the light that passed through the curtains played over her face, and in one breath told her everything.

When he was through she sat up, shedding the sheets like water.

In her eyes, that knife-edge glint.

—We could leave, she said. Go away.

He rolled onto his side and put his hand on her smooth calf.

—It'd have to be pretty damn far.

—I know a place, she smiled.

—Don't you start that island.

—Why not, Rule? Let's go. You've got the money.

—I got half the money.

—Rule, why the hell not?

—First, I don't speak French, he said and when Augustine didn't laugh he turned his words serious to match. Second, he said, you got the United States Marines there. You want to deal with that?

—We've got them here too. You think we're any less occupied here than there? Here we got ones in uniform and ones who you can't tell until they're on you. At least on *that island* you can see them for what they are.

—There's other places, he said. There's people going north.

—You don't get it, she said. Whatever way we go, it's all South.

She'd spoken without stirring and he lay before her as you might at the foot of a boulder, something immovable and defiant of the forces that would wear it down. When he shut his eyes Rule thought of rocks turned seaward and lashed with waves. He thought of black voices speaking in another language, let himself imagine them as little pieces of her voice, Augustine's voice, so that he wouldn't be a stranger there at all but becoming more a part of her. He saw himself on a green hillside, mist rolling slowly past him and down into a richer valley. Now, curled beside this woman whose country and tongue were not his own, in a small, close room, air stale with sweat and liquor and smoke, in a shabby corner of a city overseen by stone Confederates and monuments to the murderers of men like him, Rule saw his life and what it could be.

—All right.

—All right?

—Yeah, he said. Let's do it.

Before he could raise himself to meet her eyes she'd swept over him. She made no effort to hem her voice, and in the morning she was readying her bags and he was buying his ticket to Mississippi.

◆ ◆ ◆

One day as he was dying, thoughts of his wife had come swooping hawklike down on Joseph Woolsack and the racing, frightened thing his brain had become; the next day his body suddenly remembered its capacity for desire and he was stricken with want for her for the first time in years. Then he was sapped, weak, and someone had to put him to bed. Hours then of hacking, choked for air. He passed through waves of pain, chips of ice burning like coals on his tongue. And he saw the submarine that had been dredged out of Bayou Saint Jean, which he'd seen scuttled as a child on the day of the invasion, and which he'd brought his own children to see fifteen years later. This wonder, among the great mysteries of his life. He saw his children rushing ahead of him, trampling the grass and the bursts of white star chickweed on their way to the iron black thing that stood at the edge of the water like a portal to his own childhood. (Now the seas were full of submarines and Joseph had lately taken a rather inordinate and unpatriotic pleasure in this fact.) He woke from this vision and rolled over and asked his son, Red, if he remembered that day. The boy had not been born yet, Joseph realized, but was pleased when he said that he did remember. Of all his children, how strange that this was the most loyal, the most caring. If only, Joseph thought, they'd stop putting coals in my mouth. Another night and his throat was filling with phlegm and he remembered crossing the bar at San Juan del Norte, south of the Miskito in Nicaragua, in a too-small whaleboat with a fool captain who said he'd be damned if some native nigger would pilot him to shore; the boat flipping and Joseph washed to the bar, gasping, trying to stand in the shifting sand as he watched the upturned boat, the captain and his men clinging, carried toward the breakers; the water rising all around him, waves breaking over his head, filling his nose, his throat; he cannot breathe; turning to face the shore and seeing the beachfront and the palms bending in the wind, this giving onto a familiar marshland to his left, almost like home; sure that he would die, and being without children yet, he thought only of Marina. Now, many years later, drowning in his bed, there would be no boat from onshore to come and save him. And with what remained of his breath he shouted for his son, for whoever was there, to give him the pistol.

This was the other great mystery of his life: his long search for the pistol his father had used to commit suicide. The thing had in fact belonged to Joseph, a gift from father to son, specially made and engraved with his name. That his father had chosen his (of all the old man's trove of firearms) would mark him all his days, and the pistol, first hidden by his mother, then confiscated along with the other guns by Union troops, would be something he hunted, as if it held the answer. So from the time he was fifteen he'd begun to take long walks into the city and haunted the shops of pawnbrokers and gun dealers, telling no one why he went or what he searched for. When he traveled north he did the same, thinking perhaps a young soldier had brought the pistol home as a prize. And then it became such a habit that there was nowhere Joseph Woolsack visited that he didn't stop by some dusty shop and peer among the cases. He finally told someone: Angel, his oldest son, then a young man just out of school. He admitted it as you might any addiction, with great reluctance and no small amount of fear. He could see the worry in the boy's face when he told him, could damn near see the thought burning in his son's mind: You'll use it too, won't you. But Angel had been a good son then and placed advertisements and sought out dealers, chased down leads that proved fruitless. All for nothing and now that son was gone, his daughter gone, and the child beside him didn't listen but kept putting coals on his tongue.

When the doctor came to pronounce Joseph Woolsack dead, he was at first confronted by the sight of the dead man's son, who looked no less feverish and stricken. The doctor sat the man down and touched for his pulse, his temperature, and in that moment glanced from son to father and realized the wild look wasn't sickness, wasn't something caught, but rather must have been a familial trait. Something passed down in the blood.

PART 6

Prisoners

1918 – 1919

One

Looking out from a great distance onto the prairies of the Middle West, in the dead last days of 1918, you would see the wood and steel veins of railroads stand empty for days at a time. The once-busy tracks are walked by packs of dogs heading south, small bands overseen by a last few half-frozen birds that cling to sagging phone lines. A stillness and a peace that only comes in the absence of human beings, and which absence only comes when human beings are dead or otherwise distracted; the quiet broken now and then only by trains bearing shipments of troops, remnants that would hurtle by and be gone sudden as a storm, the only movement deemed essential at this time of war and, now, pandemic. What the United States facetiously calls its heartland is where the influenza first hits home. In Haskell County, Kansas. The young dying by the hundreds, the old for the most part spared. A storm in the body: first you burn, then you drown. The fourth horseman on the plains in October of 1918. (Within six weeks New York falls under quarantine.) And he is still riding even as the New Year breaks.

Isaac peering through the slats of the boxcar at still towns and farmland rolling past. Scattered on the straw floor of the bucking car sat twelve other men, prisoners like himself, some sleeping, some playing cards, others looking out. Taking every scrap of earth and movement that they could, knowing just what they were headed for. A pale band of sky, slim as hope, crushed between the dark earth and the lowering clouds, the rainfall only coming harder on the last leg to the United States Military Prison at Fort Leavenworth.

When they reached the prison depot, herded into the back of the truck that would take them to the disciplinary barrack, the rain had frozen and fell as hail. A steady pelting of the tarp that whapped over the heads of the twelve men, prisoners, more than half of them long-jawed Christian farmboys variously bearded according to their sects, the other half made up of fellow travelers, I.W.W. men, socialists, and Isaac Patterson, of no set creed and something of a ghost among the true believers. His sentence, fifteen years. Through the half-fastened flaps of the truck he watched the road unreel skittering with hail under the floodlights, the air so dark he couldn't tell whether it was night or day.

Hooded guards with lanterns led them over a footbridge to the entrance of what none of them could have taken in full, the prison a monstrous wave of stone ready to break over them.

They were brought through a series of corridors and cages, passing a clock behind its own wire cage to the office of the yard sergeant. There, with some twenty other new arrivals, they were ordered to strip, and their piled clothes were swept off as they stood naked, waiting this way until they were put into lines and marched to another room where they were measured and given ashen uniforms stamped with numbers colored according to their crimes, which a tired-looking non-com read aloud from a little book.

—Patterson, Isaac. 1296. Violation section 65, United States Code of Military Justice. Fifteen years at labor.

Isaac looked from the numbers that crossed his chest, his cuffs, his pantslegs, to those of the men around him. The numbers stood in stark relief against the gray sea of men. Scrawls of brightness. For a wild moment he imagined the numbers to be like dates, far into the future or past, and the men who wore them travelers awaiting passages to other times.

Before evening mess they were taken to the chapel and arrayed in pews before a cleric who delivered a speech from rote until he caught sight of the men with white numbers, and he paused in his speech to assure them that, while this was a place of hope and penitence for ordinary sins, those who had refused to take part in this holiest of holy wars would have neither his pity nor the Lord's.

The objectors were pared from the others and were quartered in the basement of the seventh wing. A long, low room the doors of which were left open and the men were able to move about for the time being. Mennonites seeing others of their kind gave yelps of joy, as did Hutterites and other Christians, and the socialists gathered together and shared news. Isaac could find no comfort with Christ nor with the Revolution and dead czars, and so sat off alone. He'd brought no letters, no photograph of his wife, no Bible. It had been a year since he'd last drawn. He was as alien to himself as he was to the others in the wing.

At nine the room orderly, a thin prisoner with a sawed-off broomstick in his belt, came and took the count. Coughing as he did so. Whispers now about the number sick with 'flu. And Isaac stood before his cell with his wrists crossed, waiting for his number to be called.

The following morning, after roll and a breakfast of pale gravy and bread, a thousand men ranked in the dim dininghall facing the officer of the day, when the others went off to their work in the factory or fields or the stoneyard, the new arrivals were sent into the far wings of the prison, up countless stairs and through countless cages, to be assessed in body and mind. They came to a tiled hall that opened on a dank shower room and were told to wait. While they stood, an orderly went among them asking questions.

—Any of you boys Jehovah's?

None knew what this was.

—Any of you have a problem with your blood being taken?

—For what, one said.

—For the doctors to test.

—What for?

—Syphilis, shithead.

Near the door of the examination room, a tall Mennonite boy stood with his hand raised sheepishly. The orderly looked him over—his lank blondeness, his baleful eyes.

—What's the problem, son? It against your religion or whatever?

—No, sir, the Mennonite said in his labored English. I don't like . . . a . . . needle.

A ripple of laughter in the line. Elbows prodding.

—Well, son, the orderly said. You're out of luck. The orderly turned to the rest of the line. *Anybody* who says no is out of luck, because if you do they'll just strap you down and jab a spike in your spine. Works the same way, I hear.

The showers spat cold water and the men shivered, clutched themselves, cursing. The Mennonite had to be prodded back under the showerhead and when the cold hit him he bayed so that it echoed in the tiled walls of the room, and to Isaac he looked like a bearded, long-faced dog. A voice, then another, said for him to shut the fuck up, and he did.

The men were led naked into another tiled hall, followed a stream of greasy yellow light into the bleakness of the examination room. There

Isaac, like the others, had his blood drawn, his tongue depressed, his asscheeks spread and a finger swept within. Some men tried to joke, but Isaac was past that too. They were given their clothes back, dressed, and the sick were taken to the side and the others separated by the color of their numbers, with the white numbers being sent to the psychiatrist's office, a wire-frame room that lay before a series of gates barring off the madmen's wing.

Isaac shuffled in line, drifting from himself and the body that, to his disgust, remembered well such movements and ordered days from the Baptist Boys' Home in Florida. Knew how to stand at attention, stand in line, how to look when spoken to. How to look away. He drifted somewhere above himself and tried not to think of what he had believed to be his life but was now only a gap in time between confinements. A dream. A reprieve he evidently did not deserve.

The caged bulbs cast a sour-milk light on the men in white numbers. The bearded Christians mumbling the verses they would quote in response to the psychiatrist's questions. A murmured current of thous and shalts not so different than the maniac noises that came now and then from deep in the wing. As though they were lined up to meet judgement at the gates of heaven and not a prison madhouse, and Isaac thought for a moment of asking one of the Mennonites or Dunkers how this place matched their idea of heaven.

When his turn came Isaac sat crosslegged before the psychiatrist's desk. The doctor, a man his age who by chance had gone to Tulane, smoked cigarettes and asked questions that had been put to Isaac before.

—Do you use liquor? Tobacco?

—Sure.

The doctor lit another cigarette from a table-lighter made of black stone shaped like an egg, Isaac catching his reflection in the gleam and wishing he hadn't.

—Do you use profane language?

—Do we really need to do this?

—It says here you're an artist. What did you paint?

—Pictures.

The doctor looked at him wearily.

—Abstracts, Isaac said.

—Modern.

—Yes.

—Do you belong to the Socialist Party?

—I'm a registered Democrat.

—Do you belong to a church?

—No.

—Do you believe in God?

—No.

—Are you afraid of what will happen to you when you die?

—Not as much as I used to be.

—Are you being sarcastic?

—I wish I was, Isaac said.

The doctor had the egg again in his hand, hefting its weight.

—Have you lived a pure sexual life?

—The first time they asked me I gave honest answers, Isaac said. Now I'm just wondering what you mean by that. A pure life.

—Have you committed any unnatural sexual acts? Do you struggle with unnatural urges?

—When I was a boy I was told I'd be tortured for all eternity if I touched myself.

—Do you still masturbate?

—For Christ's sake.

—Do you get angry often?

—More and more.

—Which side do you want to win the war?

—Ours.

—Which is?

—The United States.

—Good, the doctor said. But you're here, aren't you. Do you believe you can do more good by not fighting for your country?

—I think nobody's got the right to make someone kill for something they don't believe in and make heroes out of men who do. I think ten million dead men's plenty.

—But you care for your country. America is your home.

—I'm from Mississippi.

The doctor grinned.

—What if your home was being robbed, he said. Would you strike the man who tried to rob it, if you could?

—It's not the same—Isaac stopped himself. —Look, you've got my answers right there in the file. You know what I've said.

The doctor set down his egg.

—What if a nigger attacked your mother, the doctor said. Would you strike him to stop him?

—Attacked.

—Raped, then, the doctor said. What if a nigger was raping your mother? Would you hit him?

—My mother died while I was in the stockade at Fort Kerry, Oklahoma, three . . . four months ago.

—Sorry to hear that, the doctor said. What about your wife? What if she was being raped—

—By a nigger.

—If you like.

Isaac leaned forward in his seat. The black egg lay on the table, within reach. Begging.

—You want to know what I think, he said.

—Obviously, the doctor replied. The real religious cases say they wouldn't lift a hand. The socialists ask if the rapist is a union man. No private property, you know. But you . . . you're something different. So, yes, I'd like to know.

Isaac held tight to the arms of the chair.

—I think you people deserve your goddamn war and every one that comes after it.

T wo

His hands were cuffed and he was dragged to the subbasement of the seventh wing and thrown in a cell whose opening was narrower than his shoulders so that he had to go in sideways. The guard who'd brought him shut the barred door and told Isaac to turn and face front, and he did, seeing now the other men in the cages than ran on either side of him.

The guard said for him to stretch up high.

Isaac on the balls of his feet, straining to reach the crossbar in the cell door with his cuffed hands as the guard fumbled with his keyring and undid the cuff from Isaac's left wrist and looped the chain around the upright bar.

—Keep that left hand there, the guard said, letting his keys drop and hooking the cuff closed again on Isaac's free wrist.

He listened then with his head down while the guard spoke warnings and rules, and when the man left he was still hanging from the bars of his cage. He would remain this way, providing he didn't shout or talk back or trouble the room orderly, who sat at the end of the hall beneath the only light, an oil lamp, for nine hours a day for the next two weeks. If he didn't, they would bolt a wooden door over his cage that would seal him up in darkness.

The others in that ward were six communists who'd refused any work in the prison and two Mennonites, one of whom was the boy who'd bayed in the shower. Later the men would speak and Isaac would know who was down there with him, but for now he stood shackled and the world before him was the patch of stone floor barely visible. His shoulders had begun to burn. He recalled paintings of saints in similar poses. Their upturned eyes, their idiot ecstasy.

He tried, as he had so many times before, to raise himself above this. To find something to keep him whole.

As he'd tried at Camp Kirby Smith, in north Louisiana, where he was sent shortly after his arrest; a patchwork cantonment filled with recruits dressed in overalls for in the war-rush there had been no time to make sufficient uniforms, and these boys, country children oversized and full of ire, singled him for a coward; then days of wariness and small combats; Isaac refusing to drill, to muster, to do anything at all; his mail given special attention by the camp censor, so that one day in March Isaac, trembling, held a letter written by his mother telling him she had been diagnosed with a cancer of the breast (his terse letters home to his wife and family were spared for they had nothing in them, not even hope); in the end, when he was set upon in broad daylight by a troop of boys all full of bloodlust, silent as they held him down and emptied a can of yellow paint over his head, the thick, canary paint pouring out the mouth of the can somehow reminded him of his life (the officers who looked on had yet to encounter any objectors and were much relieved when this one was finally taken off their hands).

As he tried at Fort Kerry in Oklahoma where he was barracked with seven other objectors in what was called a secondary development unit; days heading out with them to haul trash for burning or to the fields with farmtools, nervously awaiting the black-barred letters and the arrival in June of the review board, a sort of traveling inquisition that determined the fate of objectors. You might be granted a furlough or some dispensation, sent to work on a farm in the Midwest, or you might be shipped to Alcatraz or Leavenworth.

As he tried when the letters from home were withheld at the behest of the camp commandant, a killer of Filipinos who was sick of coddling these cowards, so that weeks passed without a word from home and Isaac's pleas for news arrived long after the answers reached him.

As he'd tried when the board of review came and judged the depth of his convictions and granted him a farm furlough and approved his petition to go home to Mississippi for a week.

As he'd tried when the administering of the furloughs was left to the major and Isaac became a dog, all salutes and sirs, asking whenever he could about the state of his petition, which remained on the major's desk as the months wore on.

As he tried when the letter from his father came in late July, telling Isaac of his mother's death. (The letter had been written in June and told how she'd read his last, about the furlough, how happy it had made her, though in truth Mr. Patterson had read it to her as she lay insensate in bed, swollen from the cancer, so filled with morphine she could hardly nod; but he did this for the sake of his youngest son's heart, and for that of his own, which could only bear so much and would cease to beat not long thereafter).

As he tried when, that same month, a bundle of letters came from Kemper, who'd been there when his mother died. She wrote, delicately as she could, that his brother wanted no more letters from him and had sent Kemper from the house. He set the letter down and from that day forward he did not try: he gave no salutes; he hauled no trash; he went to no farmer's field. Isaac sat on his cot and refused to move, told the sergeant sent to collect him to get fucked. A moment then of violence and abandonment. When he awoke he was lying on his side in the baking sun on the dirt floor of the stockade. Walls of wire all around him, his aching head lay against the red Port soil, watching boots go by.

He tried once more and failed. His eyes had unfocused so that he could not see the bars anymore. He stared at the floor. The glow of the orderly's lamp ebbing at the edge of the dark. He watched the light swim across the stone, in danger of being consumed by the dark. The only thing left that they could take away was light.

Each day, while they were shackled, the communists talked politics in various languages so that it didn't matter if their words were overheard, but when one of them was near breaking they spoke in English of homes, women, food. Someone had told them to eat only the crusts of the bread they were given, saying that the soft center would foul their digestion, so they were scraggly things when Isaac saw them after the first week, when they were all taken to shower and shave. The young Mennonite leaned silently against the tiled wall under the bursts of water. His fellow beside him, waiting to catch him should he slip. These two spoke of God mostly but also of their homes and crops. Iowa. Missouri. Of German dishes whose names gleamed with pork fat. At night they lay on their stone bunks, eaten by bedbugs, hanging one limp arm and then the other over the lip of the bunk to let the blood flow.

On the seventh day an officer came and spoke to them, saying that anyone who agreed to work would leave solitary that day. None stirred, but at roll the following morning three of the communists and the older Mennonite decided they had proven their point and were released. That night the remaining communists sang I.W.W. hymns in French and the young Mennonite took up a psalm Isaac could not recall and which, even if he'd known it, would not have moved him.

On the eighth day he could not stop shaking.

On the ninth day the pain gained its own voice.

Afternoon of the eleventh day a party of officers' wives, fat things in Sunday dresses and fur mufflers, were ushered by a drunk lieutenant down into the subbasement of the seventh wing and they walked giggling from cell to cell, peering into the cages. They whispered among themselves, saying nothing to the prisoners, not even the young Mennonite, who wished them a blessed day. Their escort carried a lamp, and the light, coming nearer, was blinding, so that Isaac hung from the bar of his cage and could just make out their shapes.

—Well, they said.

—My, my, they said.

His pain was louder than their voices, the lamplight like the sun as they came closer. He turned away to his patch of floor, dazed. Smell of perfume and animal skin and whiskey. These wives, mothers, American furies come to judge him. And now unbidden thoughts of his wife, of his mouth pressed against her hair. Her voice. Telling him that he was all right.

The blaze dimming as the wives and their escorts went back the way they came. A man's voice saying that, if he could, he'd go through this hall with a shotgun. The women murmuring as if to say, Oh, you know how men are. Isaac thinking, Do it. Then as swiftly as they'd come the party was gone and their light with them.

On the twelfth day he started seeing things in the dark, swirling, and the things spoke. He couldn't summon his wife's voice, her face, nor anyone else he'd known. In the evening when they undid his shackles he crumpled to the floor and lay there for a long time. His tin plate and cup came scraping through the slot in the door and he did not move.

That night he woke to a voice calling his name. He sat up in his bunk, limbs drawn close with cold, unsure whether the voice was real or imagined until he heard it speak again.

—You were talking, the young Mennonite said. Are you all right?

Isaac grunted. He clasped his legs and let his forehead rest on his knees. Lately his breathing had been pained and shallow, like his chest was being filled with concrete.

—What are you still doing here? he said.

—I want to be true to myself, the Mennonite said. And true to God.

—You think you're going to get some reward for this.

—No, the boy said hurriedly. God gets the reward. Suffering . . . righteous suffering . . . can bring glory to Him. The Mennonite paused and Isaac imagined him stroking his beard.

—Running low on glory is he?

—I know you don't believe.

—I'm sorry, Isaac said.

The Mennonite spoke as though he sensed the breaking of Isaac's spirit was at hand, which it was:

—So, he said. It's only two more days we have. That's a good thing, eh?

Isaac sat quietly reckoning this length of time, his mind drifting back to earlier in their talk.

—I'll tell you what I do believe, Isaac said.

—What.

—I don't believe there's a purpose to suffering.

The Mennonite considered this for a moment. Then he said,

—Then why are you here?

Three

In the morning at roll Isaac rose from his bed like always and came forward with his wrists crossed one over the other. But now the way ahead of him took a sudden tilt, like a ship in a crosswave, and he was thrown to the ground. A brightness burning in his skull and something warm and wet spreading across his thighs. He felt more than heard through the walls of the prison a series of explosions, long low rumbles like thunder echoing through the stone. Not strength enough to do much more than claw feebly for a handhold and to groan. Life fleeing him like the light and he without the strength to give it chase.

The room orderly found him this way on the floor of his cell and went to fetch help, and he was carried past the Mennonite and the remaining socialists as the noise from above and all around grew louder. The men in their cages seeing Isaac go by were sure, each in their way, that they were witnessing a preview of their own deaths. Then he was gone and the sound was everywhere. Boilers maybe or the powerhouse gone haywire. Only when the door that led upstairs was flung open by the men carrying Isaac out did they understand the sound was made by human bodies: voices calling out, feet stamping. The sound traveled the walls and they felt the vibrations through their shackled wrists and the bars of their cages. As it happens, none of them would die in Leavenworth. The Mennonite would return to his family's land and farm it into his old age, his heart giving out one night in bed so that his wife awoke beside a stone. Of the socialists, one became a professor and endured the inquisitions of the next quarter century and the other disappeared from all account, except that he helped a former president of the Industrial Workers of the World escape while out on appeal and make his way to Russia, where the labor leader died of a stroke in a workers' hospital amid what the writer Isaac Babel would call the stunted life of the starved post-Revolution. It is not difficult to imagine a similar fate for the socialist, though there were no shortage of purges also to claim him.

When Isaac woke again he was sure they'd brought him to the maniacs' ward. All around him the occupants of the other cots were rising up and cheering, shaking the iron frames of their beds, and those who could stand clasping each other's hands, bare scrawny knees lifted in dance. He lay back, wrapped himself in the white hospital sheets and tried not to draw attention. Only when a pair of orderlies came by arm in arm, hollering between hissing pulls from a bottle of ethyl alcohol, did Isaac hear that the war was over. This was a celebration. And even then he was so feverish that he couldn't tell whether this was true or a part of the nightmare he'd been living for so long.

He learned the truth of the armistice that night, when his fever broke and he was able to sit up and take food. Then days of waiting and unease as Christmas came, rumors spreading through the prison and between the objectors most of all. Sentences reduced, pardons coming. Still he waited, not allowing himself too much hope. Letters came from Kemper, and reading her tell it helped him to believe. Not entirely, but enough. So he wrote and read and tried his best to remember the sound of her voice. Weeks later he read his wife's grim letter of late December that told of her father's death. Beneath the terse surface of her words, he sensed a frozen sea of doubt and sadness, but when he pressed her to know more she only wanted to talk about him, Isaac, coming home. Which fact Isaac couldn't bring himself to fully believe, even when, in mid-January of 1919, the quarantine was lifted and the objectors paroled out. Even when he stood in his blue serge suit and military boots on the other side of the gate and could look back at where the clothes had been made, the stacks of the prison sending columns of black smoke up into the winter sky.

◆ ◆ ◆

I see him from a distance now and then. Glancing at the shape of a passing man from where I sit at a café table or in the mull of a cinema crowd when the lights are coming up and everyone is dreamily grappling with the real, I see him. Eduard walking away, slipping on his hat, Eduard almost always hurrying somewhere, at the end of some parting, but sometimes he's pausing, and I notice how people bask in the smallness of life like dogs in the sun, or else he's doing something he'd never do, like reading at a newsvendor's rack or lighting a match with his fingernail or slicking back his hair with one hand, then I know it's not him and the lights are up in the theatre and there's nothing to do but go out into the world as it is.

The movies were a refuge. A space where we could be together for unbroken lengths of time. Of course we could find a room or he could come to wherever I was staying at the time, all the tedious drama of codes and signals that make life one long conspiracy. To love your own sex makes you the adulterer of the world, and all adulterers are runaways, ever in hiding, ever in flight. But you can't always be alone together: there's a part of you that wants to join the greater motion. No better way than sitting together watching dreams unspool on a stark white square set against the darkness. Pathé, Cineo, Edison, Eclipse. Reels of love stories from the north and of gaucho epics from the south, and, increasingly, reels of war. We'd go on weekdays, when there were crowds but not throngs, have a drink in the lobby and watch the other patrons and the ushers in their bright uniforms, then file into the theatre with them and find seats in the back but not too far, preferably against a wall, and wait in the beginnings of music for the theatre to darken and the bolt of silver light to shoot overhead through the clouds of smoke, when suddenly we'd be with people, their laughter, gasps, whispers, their shared lives.

When the poet Rubén Darío died of a punctured spleen in 1916, there was a week of funeral marches and tributes in León. Almost immediately there were calls for sculptors and monuments, even one in Masaya, a bronze, so I'm told. They have even renamed the town where he was born. Can you imagine it, for a writer in the U.S.? He'd lived in Paris in exile for years, then when the war came fled for New York, where he was taken ill. They say he wanted to come home to die. I admire that. I am coming home but not to die. I can't say what it is I'll do. I haven't seen Red in eight years, but I know enough, I've heard enough, seen enough men killed who our father would've simply bought. So I'm worried for you, sister. In wanting to be like his father and his father before him, Red's become worse.

During the week of mourning in León the poet's body lay in state, shrouded on a marble pedestal in the national cathedral. Twice a day an honor guard came to remove the shroud and change the poet's clothes. In the daylight they would dress him in the robes and laurel of some mishmash Greco-Roman philosopher, and come evening they'd dress him in a statesman's black tie. I went with Eduard to see the body, but we had to wait outside while the guard made their change. Eduard had already gone with his family, attended some events with his uncles in government, and I'd gone once before alone. But he wanted to go together, so we did. The whole time leading up to it, from the time I'd first gone to see the dead man, I was disgusted. I'd seen the poet alive a few times, heard him speak at the Pan-American Conference years before, and knowing that he was being puppeteered, changed into things neither of which he'd been, made me sick. I said as much to Eduard while we waited, whispering, but he disagreed, said in his strong, clear voice that he liked it and if he could he'd want to be remembered the same way.

"We're all more than one person," he said.

I winced. Would you believe me if I told you, after all I've written here about Eduard, that in that moment I hated him as much as I've hated anything in my life. I thought of his wife, their children, *their* life. I wanted to shout, wanted to shake him. But there were people everywhere and it was a quiet place.

"Maybe you are," I said. "You and whoever else you think you are. But I'm not."

Then I walked ahead as the guard undid the rope to let us all inside. I remember his face—Eduard's, not the dead man's. Stunned in his hurt. He hurried after me and he tried to put his hand on my shoulder but I shook it off. He had tears in his eyes, but then so did everyone else there at the foot of the pedestal. Everyone but me. I remember his eyes and how trapped he looked, unable to say what he wanted. I wanted to hurt him, and had. It didn't last long, these times never did, but still too long for me to forget.

When Eduard died I wasn't there. The city had been quarantined for months, and he'd gone to his wife and children in Managua. I couldn't even go to his funeral, as I'd gone to see the dead poet, the body disconnected from the work and the life. I could say it was out of respect for his wife, his family, but it's because I was afraid. Afraid of myself and what I would do. Were you with our father when he died? Did you speak to him? All I know comes from hearsay, small items in the news. I imagine Red was there. Mother I can't account for, even in my imaginings. The moon in the sky of my childhood, pale and distant but making regular appearances, close enough to see just how remote she was. I am the firstborn and that means I saw the ones that came after me and before you, the ghost children our parents never spoke of, though they did live, these children, and were loved, in their time. That does something to you, I'm sure. The continual destruction of hope. I am older than you, and this means nothing except that I've seen more death.

But I wasn't there with our father. The last time I saw him . . . you remember how he looked at me? Revolted and betrayed. My whole life was bound up in that look for an instant, and then destroyed. I've felt that look come over my own face and the feeling is almost as bad as the memory. I loved him, as I know you loved him. Even in better times he could be meaner than anyone I've known. I remember more than once him bringing you to tears. But then he was capable of shocking kindness too. All those days where it was only me and him, traveling, working, feeling myself filled with all his hopes. He had that way that some men have, of being so cruel that when his praise, his attention, finally came, it was the best thing you'd ever felt.

And I wasn't there for Eduard. The last time I saw him was in October of 1918. I'd just returned from an errand in Guatemala, and we arranged to meet in León. We were leaving a restaurant in the city center where we'd been drinking with friends; we'd sat for hours, talking—the first few influenza cases had come on a ship in September and nobody knew how bad it was going to be—easing back into the game of living in plain sight. It was a good time, among men we knew, but we left when the first chance came, dashing out into the rain and a hired car. We sat in the back, separated from the driver by a screen with a little portico of glass that could be opened by a latch, and when darkness filled the car from the unlit streets past the Parque Central, we were close and together and I felt as whole as one person can be. The next day he would go back to Managua, and a month later he'd be dead.

I hope this finds you, sister. I hope you'll see me, and when you do, please, don't ask me why I've come after all this time. There's never one answer to anything. I'm coming home the same way we keep on living, without knowing why.

◆ ◆ ◆

PART 7

Este viajero que ves, es tu hermano errante

1919

One

—Who the hell are you?

Isaac's voice weak as dead leaves on the frost-struck air. He'd dropped his cardboard suitcase and was leaning against the unfamiliar car parked in front of his house. Looking up at the porch, he searched the face of the man who stood there wearing a cream-colored suit and an expression that was eerily familiar. He was dark-skinned for a blonde man, and there was something in his look that made Isaac's chest go tight.

Angel Woolsack came down a step and paused when the man asked again who the hell he was. There were many ways to take such a question and Angel gave the best answer he could. Said his name.

—Kemper said you were dead.

It was then Angel realized who this man was, and for a moment they stood looking at one another across a distance of years and experience, each trying to see the other as she had.

—Do you know where she is? Angel said.

—She isn't here?

—No.

Isaac's voice was a thin string that snapped when Angel spoke. Angel watched as he began to tremble. Before he could say anything else, the man had doubled over, hands over his ears, as though he were holding his skull together.

Isaac stood again, panting, went past Angel and inside, saw the bags had been taken, along with some other things of hers, and the sight of this broke him.

Angel studied him, a suited phantom stalking through the trees and outbuildings, lashing his way through the high grass. At the edge of the marsh he screamed, cursed, bent double, and spit. Farther out the water lay in a sheet of gold, untroubled as if to rebuke his frenzy. Somewhere offshore a gull cried, its call no more sensible to the man than his to it.

What saved him was that he went into his studio, intending perhaps to burn the place down, but before doing so looked past the studies and sketches she'd kept hanging, untouched for so long, the otherworldly animals now staring back at him, and saw there in the corner the old couch wrapped in its paint-flecked blankets. He went closer and saw that the dust that covered everything else, the yellow tinge of age, hadn't claimed this place. A pillow dented by a head, blankets sunken by a body that had curled here not long before. Hers. He sunk to the floor, one arm draped over the lip of the couch. And from there he could see the folded paper wedged beneath the pillow.

He came out holding in his hand the note that told him why she'd gone and where she was going, where to find her. He went to Angel, spoke the word which in his mind was all curling shoots and blossoms reaching for the sun.

Florida.

*

210

Isaac did not find her in Pensacola, where the appearance of bubonic plague had thrown an endtimes pall over the already depleted city. Streets empty, ships in the harbor under quarantine, most businesses closed so that he had to hunt for hours for the manager of the Watkins Hotel, a sour and reluctant little fellow who Isaac begged to open up and look behind the desk for any message that had been left him. The man had been about to shut the door, but Isaac wedged his foot in the jamb and told the manager as gently as he could that this was no fucking joke.

It was noon and bright when he left with the scrap of stationery scribbled with his wife's hand, and he was smiling. He hadn't eaten for a day and a half and he'd gone from lightheaded to giddy. He walked out of the stilled city to the bluffs that overhang the bay, crossed the railroad tracks he'd wait beside for the next train, and went gingerly through the wood and scrub until he came to the edge of the forest where he felt the breath of the wind off the Gulf.

Angel had driven him to the train station, slipped a wad of money in his hand. Go find her. When Isaac asked wasn't he coming, before Angel shut the door and drove off, Angel had glanced down at the running boards and said he was going back to New Orleans, that there was something he needed to do.

Isaac rode into the panhandle through clearcut stretches and the last of the pinewoods he'd traveled as a child on foot. The train halted for water at a small station that years before had been a tavern for railmen, and he walked along the tracks toward the forward cars in the fading light of evening. Passengers dribbling out onto the wooden platform, taking a few first purposeful steps and then stopping, suddenly, having realized they were moving only for the sake of it.

There was a man with a wagon selling tours to the falls that lay only a mile and a half away, he promised, in the woods. Some passengers haggled the price and asked about how long it would take, as if they could haggle time itself, and soon a clutch of them were seated in the back of the wagon, grinning. Isaac watched them, as they went over the tracks and across the field of stumps and disappeared into the line of trees, without even a vague notion of having been there before.

It had happened like this: Under the false blue sky and the hovering ghosts, two days before Isaac would arrive home from Leavenworth, Kemper had sat and watched the black man climb down from his car. Seeing her there the man raised his hand. He was of middle height and, she saw when he came closer, heavy. Around his mouth that kind of newfound fat that takes men's faces back to boyhood. Over his gray suit he wore a coat of camel hair and when he spoke to her he didn't take off his hat.

He said his name and asked for hers and, when she answered, said plainly what her brother had paid him to do.

She froze, as people will. Searched his face, half-shadowed by the brim of his hat, and she didn't see death there. (Of course, we like to believe that we will be the ones who run, who fight, that we are too smart, too fast, too brave, for death; when in fact most people never lift a finger until it is too late, firm in the delusion that we will go on living because we can't imagine not.) Nor was it, not for her and not that day and not in the person of Rule Chandler, who had known he wouldn't kill this woman from the moment he took her brother's money. Known but had come here anyway, without quite knowing why.

—Have you ever seen me before? he said.

After a while her voice crawled out, frightened.

—I don't think so, she said.

—I was at your father's funeral. Condolences, by the way.

—Sorry, I—

—Don't be sorry to me. Wasn't my funeral.

—All right, she said, almost whispering.

—Don't worry, I won't be the one to kill you.

She sat there, gaping. Not even a thank you, he thought.

The wind came off the bay and picked up the tails of his overcoat and raised dust at his feet in the yard as he continued:

—To tell you the truth, Rule said, I don't know why I'm here. I could've just taken the money and gone, left you to find out when the next man comes.

—The next?

—Oh, I won't be the only one. He'll send another and another, I'm afraid, until the notion leaves him.

When she was done crying, her shoulders ceasing to jolt, she asked him why her brother was doing this.

—I couldn't tell you, and I wouldn't if I could. Maybe when you've got money like y'all have all that matters is wanting. Make a wish—Rule snapped his fingers—and it's done.

—What can I do?

—Run. He shrugged.

A few of the birds had wandered into the ground between them, stirring and sifting.

—You raise chickens, Rule said.

—A few, she said. For eggs.

—No rooster? What do you do about snakes? Possums?

She seemed caught off guard by the turn in their talk, struggled to form her words.

—Roosters are too much trouble, she said. Too mean.

—They can be that, he said. We had them growing up. Banty roosters, meanest little bastards you ever saw. Rule laughed. But when it matters, he said, you want a mean thing around.

She kept quiet and he considered asking her if she had a gun, of even leaving his with her, but judged he'd need it soon enough. It came to him that he cared precious little what happened to her once he was gone, providing he was not the one to do it. This was no act of justice, mind you (that fate should strike down one rich white woman didn't serve to stir his heart overmuch), but he would have his last act as an American be the refusal to do another's bidding. Somewhere in his time with Augustine he'd been able to see himself again, like an island far off in the mist, and bit by bit he was laying claim.

—You know what your brother did tell me, Rule said.

—What's that.

—He said y'all—the Woolsacks—were black. A little bit, at least, way back when. And I was looking at you just now, staring. Like it's something you can find in a face.

—It's true, supposedly.

—Well he certainly thinks so. Got very . . . you know he can get carried away . . . when he told it. I don't know what he thought it was supposed to mean to me, talking about your high-yellow grandmother like this was the secret of the world. As if . . . what? What does that make you, tragic? Does it make your story mean something?

—It doesn't mean a thing, she said.

—That's what I told him.

—What did he say to that?

—I don't know, Rule said. I was leaving, just like I'm leaving now.

Late in the night Angel slipped past the man who stood at the gate of his brother's house, lifting himself over the spikes and landing in the rear courtyard. He waited a moment, not breathing, to see if he'd been seen. Overhead a cloud-swept sliver of moon. Hearing nothing but his own heart, Angel went along in a crouch over the trimmed and dew-damp lawn and made his way inside.

Two

Angel sitting in the dark at his brother's desk. Behind him the blinds were drawn, wood tabletop stone-smooth to the touch, a pile of papers in one corner and an Emeralite lamp in the other. The house, one of those thick-walled Garden District tombs, was quiet, and while Angel waited he'd been peopling it in his mind. Hard as it was to imagine Red with a family, he'd noticed the signs on his way in. Traces of a childhood as he'd once left in a house not unlike this one. Angel's eyes had just begun to adjust when Red, or the sound of him, a rush of air, a voice, came into the room.

—Who's there?

When a person asks questions of the dark, there is a part of the asking that is not totally sincere. The default state of our minds says that no one is there. But by the sound of Red's voice, all his darknesses were densely peopled. This voice, years and octaves back, had begged him, Play with me. Angel's fingers found the beaded cord of the Emeralite and pulled it. The bulb flashed on and they faced each other in a pale green pool of light.

It took Angel a moment to grasp what he was seeing, what surrounded him. The walls of the room and even the door Red shut were papered in a pattern of overlapping crescents colored green, and gold, and black. Bananas in their stages of ripeness, a massive downpour of fruit.

While Angel sat blinking, his brother's eyes went first to Angel's hands. What the hands were doing, what they held (at the moment, nothing) concerned him more than the face of the brother he'd believed dead for almost a decade. Angel didn't know whether to be pleased or repulsed.

—When you were little, you used to steal my cleats. Wear them all over the house. Scratched the hell out of the parquet. Drove Mom and the maid crazy, but you'd clomp around all the same.

The light was like what happens in the aftermath of a storm, all milky emerald, a light that slows movement. The walls of fruit seemed to ripple and bulge.

—So, Red said.

—So I remember you, and before that, when I prayed for a little brother. When they brought you out, all wrapped up, I was proud of myself, like I was responsible. And when you scratched the floor or got blisters on your heels from shoes that were too big, I felt it too. I remember you, Red, and remembering you is the only thing that's keeping me from doing what I should.

—Which is what, Angel? Kill me?

Angel was quiet.

—Then say it, man. Say it. Say, *I'm going to kill you.*

—No.

—Say *I'm going to kill you, Red. I'm going to kill you because I can't stand who I am, because I'm jealous—*

216

—That's what you want, isn't it? A bloodbath. Fucking Greek trag-
edy. Prove to everyone just how important and grand the whole thing
was.

As he spoke Angel thought of his brother's family scattered throughout the house. What was the wife like? Did the children look like her or
like their father? Did they love him, the children, or were they terrified
of him, this father who, in death, if death were to find him tonight,
would become forever barred from them and thus infinitely important.

A long silence then as he stared at his brother surrounded by the
storm of fruit.

—Okay, Red said. Now what.

—Now you're going to sit down, right there, and we're going to talk,
Angel said. And when we're through, this'll all be over.

Three

Isaac climbing flights of hotel stairs, his breath gone. He'd found her, she was here, in a room, and he couldn't let himself entirely believe it. Now he stood before the door on which gold room numbers slanted right as if to run, as a part of him wished to do, the part that couldn't be contained any longer and might bolt down the hallway of the fourth floor of the Leon Hotel or kick down this door, which made to his mind in that moment about as much sense as raising his hand and knocking. Fear and time and loss do strange things to us; so Isaac was given pause.

The creak of bedsprings and the busying of sheets. The pad of feet over the textures of the floor, hardwood and pile, coming toward him. The door sighed with the weight of a body, leaning. Water thumping through the pipes bringing heat to some other corner of the hotel.

—Yes, she said.

Isaac urging out his voice.

—It's me, he said.

And for the first in a long time, he meant it.

In rising she had wrapped herself in bedclothes and was shawled from head to ankle, allowing only her face to show. She stood before the threshold bound in the sheets and the odors of smoke and other people, so vivid that she felt herself becoming a fraction of the greater whole whose lives had taken them through this place. And this somehow comforted Kemper when she heard her husband's small and unsure voice.

She wanted to swallow that weakened voice and feed it back to him, remade, from her tongue. She felt herself all teeth and muscle and wanted to tear him apart—the urge to consume that stalks like a wolf at the edge of love. But for the span of a few seconds, when she opened the door and saw him there, she was still.

This pale shorn version of her husband, trembling.

Her face framed in bedsheets; he would not forget this. A Klimt face framed in shabby hotel sheets, though he hadn't seen a Klimt yet and wouldn't until years later when his wife's features were retreating into the dark of forgetting. But now the shadows fled from around her, opening on the glow of her body, as she wrapped the covers like wings around him and drew him in.

The muted noises of the town outside the window, their window, stirred one then the other awake. On the floor at the foot of the bed his Leavenworth clothes lay crumpled. In a future he couldn't yet bring himself to imagine he would cut this suit for rags to dab paint and thinner, wipe away mistakes, then, still later, he would throw the rags away. He lay with her, his stomach turning for the strangeness of being touched lovingly. For so long he had been shoved and prodded and elbowed and beaten and so developed that barrier of space around him, crackling like antimatter, and now she'd broken it and he was reeling.

—Isaac.

In the window a red curl of neon signage burning dimly.

—Isaac, she said. Talk to me.

—Keep your hand there.

—Okay.

She pressed at the small of his back, the knob of spine, and held him as he fell asleep again. He'd listened to her tell what was happening, what had come to them, with a kind of abject calm.

So, he said when she came to the end, where are we going?

She hadn't realized until that moment how strong she'd grown in her time alone. Felt her strength there coiling, unsprung power. Sharp awake beside her hollowed husband—he might have been the papery husk left behind by a changing insect—she stroked his hair, saying, Far, far, away.

◆ ◆ ◆

When I was a boy our father gave me a book called *The Stranger in the Tropics*, a guidebook I used to trace his journeys and go vicariously with him. Like many pieces of my life, the book is lost now. But tonight, walking the deck as we came into the heart of the Gulf, I remembered a passage he'd underscored, an aside written in the tone of the manifestly destined, and which I committed to memory:

> *No prudent traveler should ever enter upon a journey without making provision of some conveniently portable firearm. Their use may not, and probably will not be required: but the sense of personal security and self-reliance which their possession gives, will often be of far more value than their cost. Our experience induces us also to add, in getting your arms always get the best.*

At first I smiled, remembering, but then I felt the weight of the antique pistol in my pocket. How I came by the gun, finally, is unimportant. The pistol scaled down to fit our father's hand when he was small, a present from his own father, who put it to another use. I've had the thing since before that night in Havana, when I'd been planning to give it to him as a gift. And if any good came of that night maybe it's the fact that he never got it. He'd spent long enough tending his own small museum of one family's mauled history. We all have. I tried to fire it myself once, on an unspeakable night, but found the mechanisms frozen fast.

Midnight, somewhere between Tampico and New Orleans, I was standing at the foredeck rail, the pistol in my hand. The history of any family or nation for that matter belongs to the inheritors, and this was mine whether I wanted it or not. I held it out over the railing, over the Gulf.

I try to think of what I would've said to them, to Eduard, to our father, but it's like trying to be who you were a moment or a year ago. The more you try the less comes back to you and this goes on until the last time, the one you don't see coming, when what won't come back is everything you love. Then I opened my hand and there was nothing there.

◆ ◆ ◆

Four

Later that year, in Haiti, on the road that spills and veers down the mountains from Kenscoff to Pétionville (they were headed for Port-au-Prince, some ten miles distant), Rule Chandler and his wife were riding through the clouds. He'd hitched a pair of mules (not bothering to wake his yardboys, who slept on a platform in an open stall) and started out from his house, which felt like, and once was, a fortress built against the poverty of the villages below. Augustine beside him, pale red shawl on her shoulders for the cold. The sun had only partly risen and they wanted to spend the day in town, picking up things she'd ordered for the house and so that Rule could sort out some business, both of which required her French. He had, with money and her help, acquired land to tenant out in the richer valleys to the east and servants who Augustine spoke to in a tone that shocked him when he first heard it, and the big house in the mountains, which had belonged to a now-deposed official of the arrondissement and before that a governor's brother and before that a black planter and before that a white. (Like soldier crabs, Auga joked, trading their shells.) So Rule had found himself a man of property in another country, but also a man steering mules down a dirt road, something he'd seen his father do so many times.

Before coming to Haiti, he'd never stood more than twenty feet above sea level, and after four months Rule still felt uneasy on the mountain passes, in the thin air and the crushing sky. The moment you stand at the edge and realize the mist passing over you is someone else's cloud is like the first time you realize that you are rich. On the night they arrived in Kenscoff his stomach burned and he'd felt the seams in his skull aching. Then thick grassy teas and peppery slaws were forced on him and he recovered. Gained mountain legs if not mountain lungs, but still could be struck lightheaded when rounding a bend, hugging their wagon against the scarp so that the wheels tripped stone.

Mist heavy in the pines and the drooping, dew-clung juniper, which grew thick in those days before the woods were cut clear to feed the city's need for charcoal. The way opened on ridged cropland and fields of grass lit gold where low-slung cows stood among the boulders. Rule careful with the reins as they came out of the switchbacks and onto the ridge the road followed like a spine, either side of the path a sloping tumble into cloud. There, in the clearing of the mist, he saw them coming.

A pair of men in olive on horseback, the brims of their hats, Montana Peaks, cocked askance their white faces. U.S. Marines on patrol or just wandering in the vagaries of the occupation that had begun in 1915 and would last for twenty years. A quarter mile away and coming up the road. Augustine telling him to be calm, and he had been on the few occasions they'd encountered American soldiers—feigning no English, looking away from them as though they were the sun. Now he saw the Marines had rifles across their laps and they were not clearing the way.

He halted the mules there on a strip of road not much wider than the wagon itself as the Marines came abreast and, jostling, rode up.

Rule would not be the first to speak, picked a place beyond the men to look.

The Marines exchanged a glance and one said, Will, get down and check that cart. The other, Will, scabbarded his rifle and did what the first said.

—Keep an eye on that gal, Will said over his shoulder.

The mounted one said he would, then spoke directly to Rule, gesturing around his words.

—See anybody else on the road today? *Hommes étrangers*?

Though it killed him Rule gave his head a doggish tilt, saying, *Non, non*. As he did he felt the pistol he wore beneath his coat, hard and nudging his hip. Felt its insistence but also saw himself dead by the side of the road, Auga alone. He tried, without moving his head, to watch the Marine who'd gotten down.

—We're looking for six men, the mounted one said, counting it out on his fingers. *Mal hommes. Très très mal*. Bandits, no?

Rule was shaking his head, feeling the presence of the other solider stirring now in the wagonbed, lifting the tarp, felt the man's eyes traveling up Augustine's back, and he'd turned to watch him when he heard the sound like the snapping of a green branch.

When he looked to the road he saw the Marine still mounted for a moment, eyes huge, a cane knife grown from both ends of his neck. Then olive drab awash with blood and the horse beneath him unmoving as the Marine's rifle was taken carefully out of his hands and he tilted to one side and slid into the arms of the men who'd appeared from out of the mist. Rule counted five. Black men in loose ragged pants, some shirtless despite the cold, they held the reins of the horses and eased the body of the Marine to the ground. The silent, perfect motion of a moment. Now the shock had broken and the other Marine was shouting

No and scrambling down from the wagon reaching for his hip as he ran forward. He fell with Rule's bullet in his back and lay moaning, legs in the road and his body hanging over the edge as the echo of the shot went the length of the valleys and returned. Rule had flung one hand over Augustine's chest and he could feel her heart pounding. The men in the road said nothing to him or each other, only moved as if their every motion was agreed upon before, two holding the horses while another pair went to attend the man Rule shot. This left a tall and shirtless man with long brittle hairs trying at his chin and moustache, who strode up to Rule and stared at him with smoking eyes.

He'd lowered the pistol. The man's chest and trunk were home to scars of all patterns and his ribs rose and fell without the sound of breath.

—*Americain?*

—*Wi.*

The man with the smoking eyes nodded and made a noise at the roof of his mouth and the pair came carrying the shot Marine, who they draped along with his fellow over their saddles, then returned to their leader with the pair of carbines, which he slung each over a shoulder. Then the man gave a last look at Rule before he and his men passed back into the mist. Rule sat trembling with shock and outrage for a moment when a boy appeared with fern frond bundles in his hands and swept the dirt clean in careful strokes as he crossed the road and disappeared.

Augustine was slapping at his hand.

—Go, she hissed. Go.

She didn't say another word until they were in Pétionville and that was to the postmaster. She would never look at Rule the same again, which is not to say she loved him any less but that this other side of him had come like something that swept out of the sky and she couldn't forget it. She now imagined it circling out of eyeshot, always.

They survived that day on the ridge road and would survive the occupation and later incursions and purges, and though only one of their sons would survive the Duvaliers, their grandchildren would be there for the next American invasion in 1993 and their great-grandchildren, born in Liberty City, Miami, would return as missionaries when the earthquake struck almost a century later. And Rule Chandler might have seen it all from that great height on the ridge, his head dizzy with the whirl of time.

Five

In the morning they were moving, the Packard steaming and choking over roads whose pavements ended and became long stretches of shell and gravel and then sand. Isaac had brightened some, smiled at her now and then, his hand finding hers on the steering wheel, but at other times, when the road stretched long and vacant save for them, the hollowness returned. She watched, waited, patient with him as you might be with a child. They bought smoked fish from roadside stands and pieces of fruit; parked in empty fields and slept in the open air.

Down the throat of Florida, winter a brittle, hollow skin filled suddenly with warmth. A ways outside of Gainesville, the roadside lined with shambling men chained about the ankles, prisoners hacking at the grass. When she glanced to him Kemper saw her husband's eyes tunnel, and he kept quiet for a long time after they'd passed the workgang and were alone again. She turned back to let him be with his thoughts, which were not of imprisonment, in fact, but of times further back, unwitting flashes of his childhood: a man's voice saying the world would end with falling stars, with the good transported to heaven and the bad left to be shackled and wracked by devils and stung by great scorpions that crawled from smoking holes in the ground. A man's voice saying this over and over, the sun rising and setting with his voice. Then woods and roads and rain, and chasing the hurt came something he couldn't place: a woman holding his hand to her mouth, kissing a pain away.

Kemper came to anticipate Isaac's lapses into silence and filled them with her voice. Her hand on his thigh. They spent a night in the village of Tarpon Springs, were drawn into a saint's feast by the Greek people who lived there, urged to dance and in their awkward passes were seen by an old woman who lived nearby, a woman formerly of Cyprus and who raised her glass and drank, knowing something of the strange and errant paths love takes you down. They went to bed drunk and Kemper said something funny as they lay in bed, and he, to her great surprise, added to it and their laughter then was new and wild. The sound of hope. He was, she thought, getting better, though it would be a long time before he resembled the man she'd known, and even then there was the needling feeling that he was something she had recreated from memory. But for now she took what she could and held back her fear and drove.

They went through Tampa and farther south, into reeking stretches of phosphate pits. The Bone Valley, as it was known. The Florida horizon shouldered by great mounds of clay, enormous clouds of dust rising from the pits where state prisoners mined the makings of fertilizer to feed the depleted soils of the tropics, veins of what had once been beings who swam here when this was the sea.

When they were in clear air again, they pulled off the road and parked. She laid her head on his shoulder and soon his fingers found her hair.

—I don't want to die, she said.

He put his mouth to her hair, spoke soft as sleep.

—Do you want to have a baby, he asked.

The laugh she gave almost broke him. Rising just a little, Kemper pressed his mouth shut.

—I said I didn't want to die, not that I want to live forever.

It was a moment before Isaac understood what she meant, in the same way he understood that they would be together for as long as they could. Then they were driving again, in silence, darting touches as the state that had yet to claim the sunshine as its own sank slowly into the sea. If you are quiet for long enough in a wild place, you come awake to the gigantic movements of your heart. That stirring you feel, nameless and constant, are the lives that are lost within your own. They are not yours to bring back or reckon with, and in fact never were.

PART 8

The Fugitive Quality

1961

Once when he was a student at the School of Design a noted painter had come to give a lecture on form. This must have been 1909 or 1910. Early fall, Providence not yet locked in snow. For two hours the painter spoke, his clear Northern voice lancing through the air of the chapel, aimed at hearts not yet awake as the young men seated before him scribbled notes or drowsed. He spoke about the spirit of Art and the true meaning of permanence. Isaac sat far in the back, carving worm-trails with his thumbnail in the wood of the facing pew. The names of the boys he sat beside, and those of his teachers, and that of the man who spoke, would all leave him someday, but at the end of his life, in the middle of the twentieth century, when the birds were dying and the world was deep in its slow, rasping collapse, something the teacher said returned to him.

The man had been talking about permanence of line and gave the example of a lesser-known master, some Italian, whose self-portrait hung in the Louvre. In three hundred years of storage and display, the portrait had been so mishandled and scarred that the master's face looked out at you through a web of mauling: smoke-stains and blistering, lines crackling at their edges like scars that were never stitched. And yet, the painter asked, had this destruction, great as it was, ruined the work?

No, he said. The master's line, his forms, are so powerful that they carry through the obliterated place.

Isaac had for many years laid down layers of scarring over his former life. During the latter half of the 1930s he haunted shanty camps and the dead acres of port towns. He drank himself mindless for a time in the company of other desolate men, woke one morning to find a fellow screaming for light though the sun fell full on his face. The night before the man had tapped the fueltank of a Model T and carried back a pan of denatured alcohol to their camp. Blinded now, his eyes rolled wild and pleading. He died soon thereafter and the camp broke up, some gone in pairs like roadside dogs and others, like Isaac, alone.

Days and nights spent prowling docks and then within the holds of merchant ships. He saw far countries, cities to the north whose machinery had halted as if spellcast, and southward, towns beyond poverty, where the Depression had reigned long before it had a name. He left no mark and all he owned he carried with him.

Of that period no work of his survives. The last time he touched paint had been the archway mural of a public library on the Mississippi coast, a W.P.A. project given him thanks to the entreaties of a few remaining New Orleans admirers, those who remembered the promise of his early days, and a letter forged by his wife in the guise of an eminent critic. They had, he and Kemper, returned to the United States in February of 1932, their money run thin after years abroad, and she hoped this mural would wake something in him that had been dormant for a long time. The flash of life she'd loved when they first met.

The library mural, the last of his paid work, had been intended as an ode to the workers of the region, the industry of their land and bodies, but those who came to watch the work saw a few scarce human figures (and one of these a black man, and another a Native) crowded out by patterned forms of animals like waves washing over them, repetitions of crawling, leaping, swimming things. The furtive man on his scaffold answered no questions and his wife was no better, so a band of irritated taxpayers petitioned the Works Progress Administration to have him removed. And he was, or at least he would have been. The local administrator arrived in Biloxi to find the worksite already abandoned, the painter gone, and it took some wandering until the administrator could find a Mississippi taxpayer with an answer, which was that the man had disappeared shortly after the sudden death of his wife.

In fact, Kemper's death was anything but sudden. It had been with her, unknown, for all her life. Lived in the orbit of her skull, in the lachrymal arch of her right eye, the place of tears. Nestled in webs of nerve and pressing glands that made her weep sometimes, and, rarer, gave her milk, it started as tissue the size of a pinhead. When it killed her, the tumor had grown to the size of a newborn's heart. She had in the past complained of dark patches, doubles, blurs. What doctors they visited found nothing. Then one day on the water she pointed out a small sailboat scudding toward them, not fifty feet away. Isaac's eyes had narrowed and he turned to her bemused. There was no boat, he said, just birds and pilings. When she looked again the boat was still there, firm in form, but had halted, and it set there as though at anchor until she looked away. Lying to herself and to him, she laughed, joked about glasses, but beneath it all Kemper wondered how long she'd been seeing things that weren't there. She put her fear away and tried to rest while he worked on the mural, until the afternoon when she was beside him in the car, riding home.

What happened lasted for less than five minutes, but was enlarged by time and guilt to come. The last sunlight racing them down the coast, Isaac tired from the day spent in the library arch, his neck throbbing, so that at first he didn't notice how she held her head and sighed. Kemper said she had a headache and he said the last thing he could be sure she heard.

We'll be home soon.

And he could be sure because she smiled, pained. He would remember that expression, the last time she owned her features. Then he looked away and a moment later heard her groan and the smell of shit hit him and he turned and saw her slump forward. He threw his arm across her chest and tried to hold her up as he whipped the car onto the shoulder of the road and braked, cracking his head against the wheel in the process. The car came to a halt in a patch of sand at the foot of a pier where, farther out, a crowd of children gathered at the legs of old men fishing. But Isaac didn't see them, he was trying to keep her up, touching her face, begging her to wake up, to tell him what was wrong, and the people didn't see him until afterwards, so he was helpless as the movements of her mouth slowed and the noise she made came from deeper and deeper in her body until it was gone.

At the end of the pier a ray had been brought up on an immense snatchhook and lay encircled by the children and the fishermen, thrashing. The children watching, silently, the death of this strange thing, a progress steady as the sunset on the water beyond them. These lives that live beneath our own, lives we do not recognize until we wrench them up into air they cannot hope to breathe, we know them only in their last great gasps and bursts of energy, which sputter finally out and leave us asking where that life has gone.

The children hailed a passing motorist who brought Isaac and Kemper to the hospital in Biloxi, where she lived, Isaac was told, for another two hours. He was not there; he had to be restrained. His veins pumped with sedative. Trapped within soft walls of calm. He woke in a sparse white room and gathered his sanity long enough to be unshackled and to oversee the burial of his wife, exactly three days later, at which point he abandoned it altogether.

He never regained it, not in any firm sense. Not in the decade of abandonment or that of labor or that of solitude. And when, after many years, he did return to the Mississippi coast, Isaac found the islands overtaken by soldiers, some devoted to the development of chemical weapons and others to the destruction of captured munitions. Cat Island, where he'd lain on blankets with Kemper watching night herons stalk out of the reeds, had been given over to training attack dogs. Driven mad by the explosions from neighboring islands, the dogs had been turned loose after V-J Day and came charging in a pack down the beach, snarling and knapping for Isaac when he banked. Later that same day, he watched from his borrowed boat as barges dumped shells and grenades in the passes, drums of mustard gas. And he saw the smoke rising from the redbrick incinerator on Horn Island, where test subjects were burned. If human beings in these latter centuries are charged with staying sane in the face of such affronts, he was not among the blind who could.

Now at the end of his life he'd taken to drawing the dead. The birds littering the beaches and the snarled turtles. The rafts of fish bobbing sideways in slicks of their own oils.

In 1961 he owned a cracker cottage at the end of a shell road on the western rim of Ochlockonee Bay in Florida, not far from where he'd lived as a child with Neda and his mother. An isolated corner of an already disregarded portion of what was slowly becoming a populous state. On his property there was a smaller shack he rented out, whose tenant that summer was a young woman who worked at the Marine Lab in Panacea.

When he'd come to the Ochlockonee in the midst of the Second World War, the islands in the bay were used for bombing practice by fat, silver B-24s. In his years of living here, he'd gained an eccentric's reputation among the local oystermen and others. He was known to howl curses at dredging crews and hunters. In 1952 he came to the marina weeping on the day the island of St. George was cut in half to form a shipping channel. From their skiffs the oystermen would see him sometimes: the old man rowing out, filthy hat set against the sun, or wading in the water off some island cut, working furiously at his clipboard, oblivious to the oystermen as if taking all the world and the life that sustained them into some futilely copious account that did not include them or himself. Like any stranger in a small place, there were stories, idle talk. But what obtained in all accounts was that this man had lived a long and unhappy life. So he was treated with deference and given the distance which seemed to be his only wish.

Between trips he worked in a small room off the back porch of his cottage, head light with the fumes of the housepaint he used in lieu of oils and which would have killed him had his death not lain elsewhere. When he could no longer stand the shore, Isaac rowed out and camped among broken trees and at the edges of blast craters that had over the years become lagoons, and he drew the dying and the dead. The abundance of life that had marked his youth had become an abundance of death, and if he couldn't accept it, if his mind cried out to know what happened to the life, to the thrash and rush of living when the living was done, he could, he told himself, make use of the forms life left behind.

In May of 1961 he went out to the east of Ochlockonee Bay to Piney Island, a green scrim four miles from shore, and fell into his accustomed pattern of work and watching. Woke on the second day and at low tide waded out past the weir of oysterbeds to a patch of grass where he thought he'd seen a bittern nest.

The night before he'd heard the bird's deep drip-drop call, seen her at sundown carrying reed-stems in her beak. Whether it was true or not in pure numbers, he believed he'd seen more dead birds than live that year. And now, more than anything, he needed life. He needed to draw the bittern's eggs, the pale green shells the atmosphere of a gold small inner world.

So, chest-deep in cool water, bare feet flushing rays and stirring grasses that sighed back to rest on the sandy bottom as he passed, he came to the patch of grass and parted it with his free hand. The bittern, flew off, and Isaac saw the nest, a spiral thatch rising from the reeds. He had his clipboard tucked under one arm, sweat staining the clasped sheets cut from the sides of grocery bags, pencil hanging from his neck as ever. Leaned closer and reached up into the mouth of the nest, willing sense into his calloused fingertips and feeling for the smooth shells. What he felt instead was a dart-sharp pain and a fire in the meat of his palm. He jerked his hand back just as the cottonmouth came spilling out of the nest in one uninterrupted pour. The snake's skin patterned like the bittern's feathers, like grass and mud, black-streaked brown and buff. Made for here. The snake slid through the reeds and swam off in the direction of land.

He'd never been bitten before. His whole life. This thought almost comic in his fogging mind, followed closely by the memory of Kemper talking to the fat old kingsnake that followed her while she gardened.

He held his hand, throbbing, against his chest, where his heart had likewise taken up a frantic, jagged beat.

Midnight the tenant who had recently started living on Isaac's property, having escaped her marriage of two years to a helicopter pilot and retreated south to spend her days before bubbling tanks of ocean life, woke to a squall that shook the walls of her shack, to windows washed with rain. It had been three days since she'd last seen the old man, and she was worried. When the storm was through she went half-dressed down the sand drive, raking her path with the beam of a flashlight. She crossed the road and came to the spit where he launched. Found nothing but sand and crab scuttle. She swept the light out over the water. A mullet leapt and fell. She thumbed the switch and stood there listening in the dark.

He'd made it to the island, dragged himself onshore, when the retching came that bent his thin body double and emptied him. In the distance his abandoned clipboard floated unnoticed, leaves reaching down into the water.

His bitten hand, leaden and dead, fell and dragged along the ground as he crawled toward his camp. He might have lain there and let it happen, let death come, but he'd become a passenger in the flight of his own body, which wanted, as bodies do, only to survive.

Isaac gained his feet, bile streaming from his lips.

The wind was coming from offshore when he made it to his camp. Found his water and drank, spat, fainted briefly. Groaning, he got his fire going in the pit, crouched over the flame to shelter it from the wind, fed it with twigs and his sketches from the day before. Then he set a pan of water in the fire and took his clasp-knife from the pack and cut a cross into his dead hand. Trembling, he sucked his own blood, which ran freely thanks to the poison. The wind at his back, his heart burning, he waited for the water to boil. Waited and fell unconscious as if through a trapdoor.

Eyes open to the glow of flame. He rose up in horror at the sight of what he'd done. The fire had been blown by the wind and spread across the island in a wave that spat smoke and small birds like burning paper. Everywhere underfoot went small, scared things. Woodrats scurrying and crabs, boar piglets burst squealing from a burning vein that had once been an oleander.

All of this, his doing. His fault.

He took his bedroll and for a long time shambled along the wave of fire, beating at it with the blanket, cursing, howling. His every movement urging the snakebite's poison on. He knew this, but kept fighting, and knowing that he would die for this, for what he'd done, was a small consolation. When the wind turned and the fire chased him back to the beach, he was crazed with poison and smoke. Weeping, Isaac shoved his boat into the surf and flung himself aboard, where he fainted again and the outgoing tide, the strongest in months, carried him to sea.

The following day the tenant reported him missing, filed a formal report with, Coast Guard and put the word out to fishermen and tourists at the dock. She stayed by the radio into the next shift as the sun bled red against the grease-flecked window overlooking the gas pump and the icemaker, watched the ships coming in the channel, expecting the next to be lashed with the old man's empty skiff. Someone said there'd been a fire on Piney Island, just before the storm, but when they ventured out the searchers found no sign of him there or on any other of the countless smaller islands along the coast.

In the end she went with a sheriff's deputy who pried open the door of the old man's house. Inside, a warren of paper and piled furniture. The tenant and the deputy had flashlights on and they were midway through the front room when she realized what the papers were. She lifted up one sheet after another to her light. A painted tern looked back at her. A pattern of gulls. The arched backs of dolphins diving through leaves of pasted butcherprint and the backs of grocery bags. They went on deeper into the house. A little space carved into the kitchen where he'd sat. The cold stove. Everywhere stacks of paint and jars of murky colors. Brushes stiff and sharp as arrows. Piled cans of housepaint. Child's sets of colored pencils and pastels cracked with age or melted. And everywhere the work.

Around this time the first mate of a United Fruit ship glassed a skiff bobbing a quarter mile parallel to their path, west of the Florida Strait. The skiff had no markings, no occupant that he could see, and he took it for the sort put out by poor fishermen and frequently lost. The ship, which carried agents of Central Intelligence and crates of rifles among the bananas, could not stop on its way to Ciudad Trujillo, say, or maybe Barranquilla. There was greater work in the world and it would only end, for that company, fourteen years and several mergers later, in midtown Manhattan, when its chief executive bolted the doors of his office on the forty-fourth floor of what was then the Pan Am Building, took his attaché case and smashed a shoulder-width hole in the tempered plate glass window, cleared the sharpest shards away, and leapt. Before coming to ground on the Park Avenue Viaduct, to the outcry of break and tire and horn, the executive's body was glimpsed in its descent by a few stunned onlookers who happened to glance that way, the hurtling man a sign of things to come.

The current carries Isaac Patterson far out into open water.

He wakes, alive, high in a swell. Dark shapes in the waves. He sleeps and believes he will die, only to wake alive again. Life startling as the dawns that break so suddenly this far out at sea. In the belly of the boat he lays facing the sky.

She comes as no surprise. Kemper. He's seen her since the day they met, in one form or another. But when he dies she will not be there, he will not see her, know her, or know where he is or what is happening. Even the Gulf becomes a stranger, as in death the elements are shorn of their associations. Wind is wind. Rain is rain. Water is water. Light nothing other than itself. The living world goes on, neither cruel nor kind but written with its nature and wanting none of us. No pleasing vision, no memory will ease him to his end. On the horizon he will never again see, clouds lower and reach out dark tendrils to the steaming surface of the sea.

They will tell you change is the nature of things. And it is the nature of certain paints to pale over time, or to darken, or to shift into another shade entirely. The fugitive quality, this is called. Much work is lost this way and that of Isaac Patterson would be no exception. Cheap watercolors and housepaints are easy prey to light and time. As it happened, the oils of his early work would last the longest. And while the colors of his life fled, men on platforms in the Gulf sent down drills tipped in diamond to bore in the bed of the sea, retrieving packed cylinders of earth as it was in other ages. These cores they carried to the headquarters of their company, which occupied a city block in New Orleans once home to a shipping and fruit concern owned by a footnote family whose name was not remembered, a brief and minor enterprise as these things go, and the cores were cut along their lengths into inch-thick hunks and arranged in sequences of time, stored in boxes of treated wood and kept in this corporate substrata for years, untouched in the dark, though they told in mineral lines that this had been the place from which the light had come. The light that came and meant the end of some lives and the dawn of others who would likewise live their time in the belief that all of this was theirs. Ours. The shriven marshlands, ours, and the nestlings choked in gouts of oil. The islands beaten into white shards like something hurled down and smashed, gone in the span of a human life. That meaningless scale by which we measure stories that will be told, in the end, not by lives or paint or words or the frail vessel of the human voice but in the layers of earth and the water that is coming to cover us whether or not we care to know.

Acknowledgments

Background:

While the action of this novel occurs in times and places that do not always correspond to the historical record, the writing of it would not have been possible without the work of many scholars and writers. Particularly Michel Gobat, René de la Pedraja, Lester D. Langley, Peter Chapman, and Susan Cerulean.

The character of Isaac was born from many artists, but among the chief inspirations was the work and life of Walter Inglis Anderson, whose art stands as a testament to the beauty and fragility of both the Gulf Coast and the human spirit. Please seek it out.

This book is for:

Two writers I have never met and who are now gone, but without whose work this book would not exist: Eduardo Galeano and Jim Harrison.

My agent, Gail Hochman, for tireless advocacy. The amazing people at Grove Atlantic: Peter Blackstock, who saves my sentences and sanity on a regular basis, and most especially John Mark Boling, Deb Seager, Elisabeth Schmitz.

Josh McCall, who knows my tics and tremors and whose editorial eye never fails.

Jim Davis, who keeps the light of literature alive in my home state.

William Bedford Clark of Texas A&M for his kindness and friendship.

Huntley Johnson, the most hardcore reader and lover of letters in these United States, for opening his home, his treasure trove of books, and most importantly his heart to me and my wife.

My hometown bookstores and the wonderful people who run them, Octavia Books and Garden District Book Shop. Special thanks to Brazos Bookstore of Houston and a pair of readers so glorious I'm not sure I deserve them, Mark Haber and Keaton Patterson.

Taylor Brown, brother from another coast.

Colleagues at Southeastern Louisiana University, all of whom are aces, in particular Chris Tusa, David Armand, Thomas Parrie, Jason Landrum, and Carin Chapman.

Bob Shacochis, for many things, but especially for the hours on the water.

My family, all of you, for generosity and love and unending tolerance for me dragging your surnames through the muck of history and my imagination.

Andrew Smith, whose friendship is one of the great gifts of my life.

My wife, Alise, who did the most amazing thing I've ever seen, and somehow manages to be more wondrous each day.

My daughter, who spent many a night wrapped against my chest while this book was being written, a constant reminder of what matters most, what all the people listed here have given to books, to art, to the natural world, to each other: love.